Swordbird

SWORDBIRD

NANCY YI FAN

ILLUSTRATIONS BY
MARK ZUG

HARPERCOLLINS*PUBLISHERS*

Swordbird

 For information address HarperCollins Children's Books, a division of HarperCollins Publishers, 1350 Avenue of the Americas, New York, NY 10019.

www.harpercollinschildrens.com

Library of Congress Cataloging-in-Publication Data

Fan, Nancy Yi.

Swordbird / Nancy Yi Fan. — 1st ed.

p. cm.

Summary: Warring factions of blue jays and cardinals call on Swordbird, the heroic bird of peace, to rescue them from the evil machinations of Turnatt, the tyrant hawk lord who plans to enslave them.

ISBN-10: 0-06-113099-0 (trade bdg.) — ISBN-13: 978-0-06-113099-1 (trade bdg.)

ISBN-10: 0-06-113100-8 (lib. bdg.) — ISBN-13: 978-0-06-113100-4 (lib. bdg.)

[1. Birds—Fiction. 2. War—Fiction.] I. Title.

PZ7.F19876Swo 2007 2006017720

[Fic]—dc22 CIP

AC

Typography by Amy Ryan

1 2 3 4 5 6 7 8 9 10

❖

First Edition

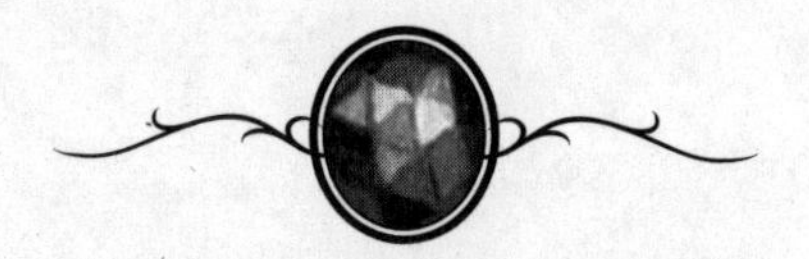

To all who love
peace and freedom

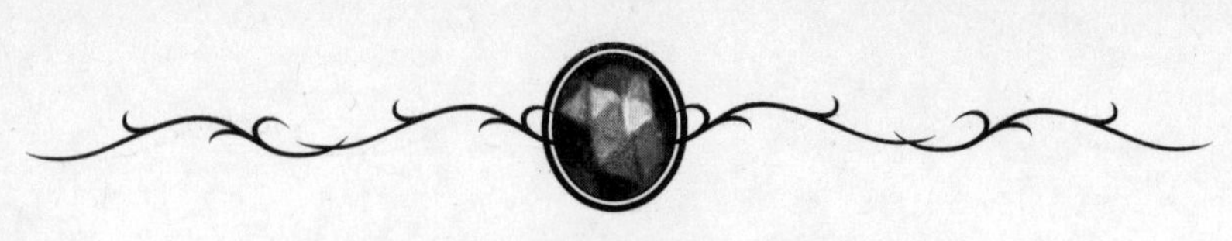

TABLE OF CONTENTS

MIRROR LAKE

PERIDOT RIVER

THE LINE

BLUEWINGLE
TRIBE
(BLUE JAYS)

APPLEBY HILLS

SUNRISE
TRIBE
(CARDINALS)

PINENUT CREEK

STONE-RUN FOREST

SILVER CREEK

TWILIGHT
LAKE

FORTRESS
GLOOMING

N
W
E
S
WHITE CAP MOUNTAINS
ROCKWELL RIVER
WATERTHORN TRIBE

SWORDBIRD

Darkness nourishes power.

—FROM THE *BOOK OF HERESY*

PROLOGUE

SHADOWS

Beams of light fell through the trees, creating shadows that flecked the thick, moist undergrowth. Hidden in a patch of those shadows, a fortress was under construction. Many woodbirds had been captured and pinioned for this, and they worked wordlessly, carrying stones, clay, and sticks day after day. Usually a coal black crow could be found strutting among them. Whenever possible, he would spring on an unsuspecting victim with curses, yells, and a sound lashing. He was Bug-eye, the driver of the slavebirds, who carried a black leather whip the color of his feathers.

Through one sly golden eye, a red-brown hawk in dark robes observed the construction of his fortress. His name was Turnatt. Large for his kind, he towered over his captain and soldiers. With sharp claws for battling, a loud, commanding voice, and foul breath, he was a bird to be feared. His nasty habit of tapping an eye patch over his left eye while glaring with his right made the other birds shiver.

Turnatt had raided countless nests, camps, and homes, capturing woodbirds as slaves and bringing them to this secret, gloomy corner. Now the time had finally come: the building of Fortress Glooming. Sitting on a temporary throne, the hawk let thoughts of evil pleasure pass through his mind. As Turnatt watched the thin, helpless slavebirds' every movement, he tore into a roasted fish so messily that juices ran down his beak.

Slime-beak, Turnatt's captain, was hopping about, glancing at the trees bordering the half-built fortress. He dreaded Turnatt, for he worried about being made into a scapegoat.

Displeased, Turnatt stared down his beak at his nervous captain, his bright eye burning a hole into the bothersome crow's face.

"Stop hopping, Slimey—you're getting on my nerves. I'll demote you if you keep on doing that." A fish scale hung from the edge of Turnatt's beak.

Slime-beak shivered like a leaf, partly because of fear and partly because of the hawk's bad breath.

"Y-yes, milord. But it has been three days since Flea-screech and the soldiers went to look for new slaves. They still haven't returned!"

The hawk lord guffawed. The tail of the roasted fish fell from his beak and disappeared down the collar of his robe.

"Fool, who has ever heard of little woodbirds killing a

crow? If you don't stop with that nonsense, I'll send *you* to get slaves! Now go and check the progress on my fortress. Then come back and report your news!" Turnatt waved the long, embroidered sleeve of his robe at the captain.

Slime-beak thought himself lucky that the hawk was in a good mood. Knowing Turnatt was fickle, Slime-beak dashed away.

Seeing the crow scurry off, dizzy and awkward, Turnatt tapped his covered eye in satisfaction. He chuckled, his glossy feathers shaking. His fierce yellow eye narrowed wickedly, becoming a slit. He was Lord Turnatt—the Evil, the Conqueror, the Slayer, and the Tyrant of soon-to-be Glooming. He thought about torturing woodbirds, killing others that got in his way. Nobird—*nobird*—could stop the mighty Turnatt. It would be as he had dreamed for seasons. He would rule the entire forest, with millions of slavebirds to bow down before him. Turnatt tilted his head back and let out a bloodcurdling screech that echoed throughout the forest. Slime-beak and the soldiers followed suit, their loud chants drowning out every other sound.

"Long live Lord Turnatt, long live the Tyrant of Fortress Glooming, long live the lord!"

Over the shouts, the sun rose above the treetops.

A forest split in two cannot stand.

—FROM THE *OLD SCRIPTURE*

1
THE RED AND THE BLUE

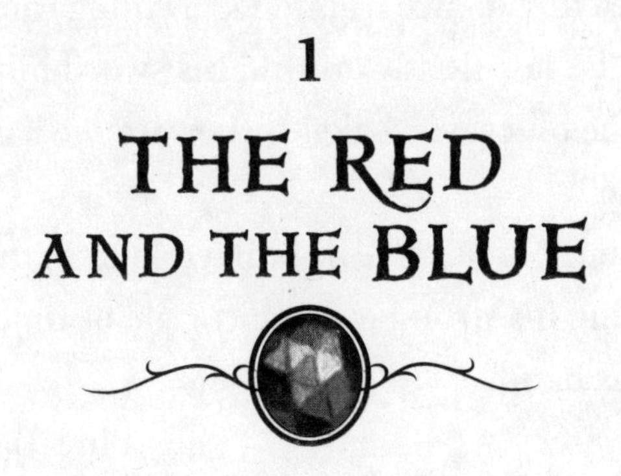

Just north of Stone-Run Forest, a war party of cardinals glided in and out of the shadows as the light of dawn slowly slipped into the sky. They traveled swiftly and low, each grimly wielding a sword in one claw. The leader, Flame-back, a sturdy cardinal distinguished by his larger and more powerful wings, reviewed their plan of attack.

"Circle the camp, wait for my signal, attack. Simple.

Everybird understand?" Crested heads bobbed in answer.

The idea of violence frightened a young cardinal, who wrapped his claw tightly around his sword hilt. "Flame-back, are the blue jays awake? If they are, we'll die! I don't want to die!"

Flame-back looked at the blurred land in the distance and, flapping his strong wings a couple of times, tried to reassure his band.

"The blue jays don't wake up so early, and nobird's going to die. Nobird's going to kill. Hear? We just scare and attack. No hurting." Pausing, Flame-back added in a more comforting tone, "And we must find our eggs. We can't let anybird, anybird at all, steal our unhatched off-spring." The speech calmed his band, especially the youngster, whose wail dwindled to a sniff and a sob.

The cardinals were deep in thought. They all knew that Flame-back was right. There were no sounds except their wings, whooshing and rustling against the wind as they flew—red figures against a blue sky. They soared over the Appleby Hills and across the Silver Creek. Dewdrops trembled on delicate blades of grass; dandelions and daisies peeped over their leaves to greet the sun. Near the fringe of the forest, beech trees stood still, and only the morning breeze occasionally disturbed them. Those trees were ancient ones, covered with moss and vines, leaning over to touch branches with one another. Small creeks gurgled gently as they rippled along, under mists that covered the ground. But the cardinals were in no mood to enjoy such things. They were on a mission. The war party made a sharp turn along a boulder and flew over the Line, the border between the territories of the blue jays and the cardinals.

As they crossed, a twinge of uneasiness ran along every cardinal's spine. They were entering forbidden territory. But about a month before, it hadn't been. A month before, the cardinals and blue jays had been good friends. Their hatchlings had played with one another; they had fished for shrimp and hunted for crickets together. But things were different now. With a brisk flap of his wings Flame-back led his cardinals through a twist in a gap in the tangled trees.

"Lively now, lads. You all know what we're here for, so get ready. Fleet-tail, branch off with a third of our forces and go around to the left. You, take another third and go to the right. The rest, follow me. Swift and silent, good and low, friends."

In a flash the cardinals separated into three groups and departed into the shadows. After flying through a ghostly fog, the cardinals saw their destination. Eyes glistened and heartbeats quickened. With a few hushed words, the cardinals swiftly got into positions surrounding the blue jay camp. No feathers rustled. They sat as silent and rigid as statues, waiting for Flame-back's signal to attack.

The cardinals' target was ten budding oak trees hidden behind a tall, thick wall of pines. The oaks grew in a small meadow of early spring flowers and clover sparkling with dew. The pine tree border was so dense that one might fly right past it and not see the oak trees inside. It was indeed cleverly hidden. Those oaks were the home of the Bluewingle tribe.

It was very quiet. Occasionally a swish of feathers and breathing broke the silence. A strange long-limbed tree protruded from the center of the grove. In the branches of this tree a hushed exchange was taking place.

An elderly blue jay, Glenagh, shifted on his perch, his thin gray shoulders hunched up. Peering through the oak leaves, he could see a dim ray of light climbing up the ancient mountains.

How long can we go on fighting our old friends? the old blue jay wondered.

He turned abruptly to face his companion, Skylion. "How are you going to keep this 'war' up?" Glenagh asked. "Ever since you became the leader of the Bluewingles, we've been fighting the cardinals constantly." The old blue jay sighed. His feathers drooped. "You definitely do make your mind up faster than a falling acorn hits the ground."

Skylion turned his gaze toward the elder, Glenagh. "They used to be our friends—our family, almost," he said. The younger blue jay poured a cup of acorn tea for the elder with disbelief.

Shaking his graying head sadly, Glenagh accepted the tea with a worn claw. He gazed at his reflection in his cup with a dreary look. "Remember Fleet-tail? The cardinal who's always so quiet? Just last week I saw him with a raiding party, hollering and yelling like the rest."

"Well," Skylion replied hoarsely, "we have to regard

the cardinals as enemies. Stealing and robbing—that's what they do now."

Leaves rustled as the wind changed direction.

"True, the cardinals have robbed us bare to our feathers, but we have done our share as well." Glenagh glanced again at the light outside. "The sack of pine seeds, the raisins, the bundles of roots, the apples . . . We've taken back more than what was stolen from us. We cannot say we aren't thieves."

Skylion hastily dismissed the idea. "Yes, but they stole our blueberries, our walnuts and honey! They stole the raspberries, the mushrooms, and more!" the blue jay leader argued. "We only took back food because we needed to survive. It's just spring. There's hardly any food you can gather outside. And what about our eggs? Our offspring. The next generation. Is there an explanation for that?"

"Peace is more important, Skylion." Glenagh shook his head and took a sip of acorn tea. "You do have a point about our eggs, but the cardinals declared that we stole *their* eggs and they didn't steal *ours*. I cannot believe that having been friends for so long, we have suddenly become enemies. Maybe they didn't steal from us; maybe somebird else did. We should go and talk with them about this."

"No, Glenagh. It would be a waste of time! We tried to talk before, but they only accused us of stealing from them first. You know that isn't true!" Skylion snorted.

"But Skylion, don't you—"

Skylion leaned forward. "Glenagh, can you stay calm and aloof when our eggs are snatched and stolen right from under our beaks? Of course not. We are fighting to get them back!"

Glenagh calmly looked at the leader, the steam of the tea brushing his face. He was silent for a few moments and then said, quite slowly, "Does fighting solve the problem?"

Skylion sighed deeply and shifted his glance to the wall, where there hung a painting of a white bird holding a sword. Though the painting was worn and the color faded, the picture still was as magnificent as ever. The bird seemed to smile at Skylion. Skylion almost imagined that the bird mouthed something to him.

Skylion whispered, "I wish Swordbird could come here to solve this."

"Ah, Swordbird . . ." Glenagh toyed with the name as a smile slowly lit up his face. "The mystical white bird, the son of the Great Spirit . . . He is a myth, but I know he exists. I know in my bones. Do you remember the story in the *Old Scripture* about a tribe of birds attacked by a python? They took out their Leasorn gem and performed a ritual to summon Swordbird. Immediately he came in a halo of light, and with a single flap of his great wings the python vanished into thin air." Glenagh paused. "Well," he said, "to call for Swordbird, we need a Leasorn gem. It's said to be a crystallized tear of the Great Spirit. But we don't have one. We have no idea where to find one either. So, it's what's in you and me that counts." Glenagh drained his cup, savoring the last drops.

Skylion opened his beak to reply, but he was interrupted by a frantic rustle of leaves. A young blue jay's head poked through, and in a high, nervous voice the youngster gave the message: "The cardinals! We are being attacked! *We are being attacked!*"

Birds are born to have wings;
wings are symbols of freedom.
—FROM THE *OLD SCRIPTURE*

2
SLAVEBIRDS' PLAN

Turnatt's horde had flown from the warm southwestern region to Stone-Run with about forty slavebirds. Because crossing the White Cap Mountains was trying and treacherous and food shortages occurred on the way, only thirty-eight slave-birds survived the trip.

A month before, the slaves had lived free among their own tribesbirds. Now they dwelled in the leaky, half-rotten slave compound, with their legs chained to a stone wall. The building's walls were wooden bars that gave off awful splinters, and it seemed as if they would collapse at any moment. Above, rotting hay and logs were bound together for a roof, with holes here and there to see the sky; below was the bare ground, always uncomfortably moist. As the mild spring brought showers and damp winds, the slaves were allowed to build a fire in the slave compound. The birds wore nothing but rags on top of their mud-caked feathers, and as they huddled around the fire, they shivered.

Tilosses, an aged sparrow who had not lost his sense of humor, started the discussion.

"It has been several weeks since we were caught and brought to this filthy place. Ladies and gentlebirds, we have no other choice: If we wish to see our homes and families again, we must escape!" Tilosses paused to make his speech more dramatic. "Escape may not come easily like a grand supper delivered to us; nevertheless, we can find a way if we work at it. That Turnatt may be dangerous, but sometimes he is as careless as a fly. *Pah!* Why, his name sounds like Turnip!" Hearty laughter followed. "We all know that we need to escape somehow, not remain here to rot. The question is, how?"

Across the campfire a burly flycatcher called Glipper

spoke up. "If just one of us escapes, we might have a better chance. The native woodbirds in this forest would help us if we can send a message to them." There were murmurs of agreement.

"Well," a nuthatch said, "the woodbirds would help us, but how can we reach them? The guards are too numerous, and that slave driver, Bug-eye, seems to be everywhere at once. It's really unsafe. How could anybird slip out of the fortress to contact the woodbirds?"

A jaunty goldfinch blurted, "I know how! Trick the captain. Make him think you're helping him. Convince him to let you gather firewood every day outside the fortress. He'll trust you after a few days. Then find a woodbird to help!"

"Good idea!" said Tilosses.

Glipper shook his head. "Chances are, nobird would be allowed outside alone," he declared. "There's little possibility of success, with all the risks and hazards."

"But there still is a possibility, however small, so we should try it," somebird in the crowd murmured.

Tilosses spoke. "Who will take the risk?"

"A bird who is wise, persuasive, and innocent. These are the right qualities," chimed the goldfinch, cocking her head to one side.

The silence stretched for a long time. A twig crackled

in the fire. *Who will do it? Who? Who?* The question hung in the air.

"I will!" The voice of a young robin piped up from the crowd of slavebirds. Heads turned to see the speaker.

Though all the slavebirds knew the robin's name, they had no more knowledge of him beyond that. He was quiet, rarely speaking to anybird.

At first glance he seemed rather weak for his kind, yet when the slavebirds took a close look at him, they noticed that his agile legs and lean frame looked strong, able to endure. He had a speck of red among his black neck feathers. Despite his bedraggled, thin, and dirty appearance, there was something in his big, shining eyes that warmed the onlookers' hearts.

"Miltin?"

The robin nodded, and the corners of his beak twitched into a smile. He looked so confident that everyone knew he should be the chosen one.

Glipper peered at the robin and grinned. “Miltin, I have a feeling that you are going to have quite some adventure.”

Outside, the wind whistled.

The supreme pleasure a tyrant
can gain is to torture others.
—FROM THE *BOOK OF HERESY*

3
Squawk, Squawk, Squawk

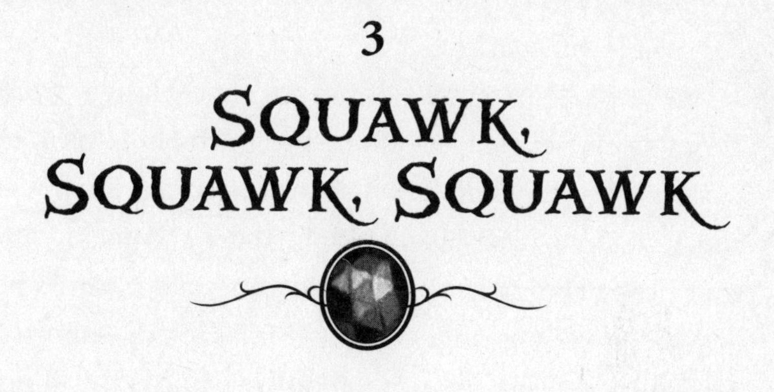

Turnatt perched side by side with his captain, Slime-beak, drinking chestnut beer and wine and talking in a newly built room of Fortress Glooming. Magnificent blades and ancient weapons glistened on the walls, soft cushions adorned chairs of red cedar, and silken curtains draped the windows.

The hawk lord glared at his captain over the rim of his silver goblet. "You'd better finish the construction of my fortress in eight weeks," he threatened, "or I'll pull your feathers off to make me a duster!"

Slime-beak cringed. "I-I'm afraid finishing is almost impossible, milord."

"What?" The flames of anger that blasted from Turnatt's eye seemed hot enough to burn Slime-beak to a crisp. "You remember, when we first came here, you and I sat down and talked? Right there and then, with your beak flapping like an old shoe, you said it would be finished in early spring. Well now! It is close to summer, and you're still nagging me about needing more time. What in the world of crazy captains is your reason?"

"Well . . . w-we're short of wings now, mi-milord. Many of the slavebirds h-have been sick." Slime-beak's voice crackled in fright as he spoke.

Because Turnatt knew that was the truth, his anger subsided a bit. He still growled slightly as he talked. "Flea-screech will bring back more slaves soon. There are cardinals and blue jays nearby. They'll make good workers. Kill the sick slavebirds as soon as we have new ones," he commanded, setting down his goblet. The silver reflected the rising sun and became blood red. "And tell the scout, Shadow, to come here."

"Yes, milord, yes, milord." Slime-beak made his exit with springy, clumsy hops. The crow captain's wings were tilted awkwardly as he walked, and the pungent smell of alcohol surrounded him like a thick mist.

As soon as Slime-beak's clawsteps faded, Shadow glided in. He was a striking raven with amber eyes instead of black. Turnatt mentioned the blue jays and cardinals to him.

"Some cardinals and blue jays, you said, Your Majesty?" Shadow bowed his head respectfully and closed an amber eye. He seemed to melt in a puddle of darkness as he twirled the edge of his black cloak fancifully with a thin, bony claw. "Aye, sire, they're north of us, not too far by the wing. We stole some food from their pitiful camps. Now each of them believes the others are thieves." The scout reopened his eye and peered at the hawk. Turnatt growled his approval. Shadow beamed as he was offered a mug of beer, and he accepted it with ten times more flair than Slime-beak had. Sipping silently, he answered with words Turnatt would like to hear. "I will check on them again today and bring back some white grapes to make fine wine for you, Your Majesty. You are too noble for such a drink as beer, Your Majesty."

"Yes, yes," Turnatt urged. The effect of the liquor was starting to make the hawk lord drowsy. "Create even more disturbance and confusion for the cardinals and the blue jays. The more the better! Then they'll be weaker when we attack!" The hawk's eyes misted slightly. "Now go, Shadow."

The raven scout dipped his tail in salute and left, his amber eyes shining with eagerness. He uttered a flattering remark as he left: "You are the mighty conquerer, Your Majesty. Farewell."

As soon as the scout faded into the shadows of the hallway, Turnatt pictured a score of cardinals and blue jays in his power. Yes, he would whip some of them himself. Maybe he would pull feathers off a blue jay to make a fan and torture a cardinal with fire, watching his feathers get scorched. . . . All the birds, his own! His own! *Squawk, squawk, squawk.* That's what the birds would cry for mercy.

Turnatt laughed out loud. "Squawk, squawk, squawk . . ." he mused, speaking to himself. "Yes, they deserve that." From a shelf nearby he took out a tome entitled the *Book of Heresy* and started to stroke the cover lovingly.

Outside the door Tilosses was eavesdropping, still wearing the apron as assistant to Turnatt's cook. He had pressed a teacup to the door and drawn his ear close to it. "Oh, yes," Tilosses said with a soft chuckle. "That's what Turnatt will say after he finds out that the slave-birds have escaped. Squawk, squawk, squawk."

What does fighting bring us?
Fear, hatred, misery, and death.
—FROM THE *OLD SCRIPTURE*

4

THE BATTLE OF THE APPLEBY HILLS

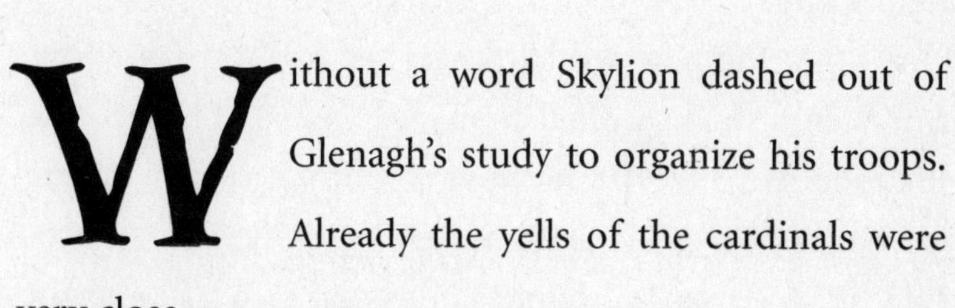

Without a word Skylion dashed out of Glenagh's study to organize his troops. Already the yells of the cardinals were very close.

"Seven to guard the food store, ten to protect the eggs and the weak birds! The rest of you, quick, form three rows, and go outside with backs to the trees! Hurry!" he hollered. The quiet halls were suddenly alive with action and noise. The blue jays took off from different perches and flew in quick formation to their assigned posts.

Skylion drew his sword and burst from the shadows of the leaves out into the daylight. "Attack! Bluewingles forever!"

They were greeted by the flashes of the cardinals' swords and loud yells.

"Power of the sun! Sunrise, charge!"

The silent morning was instantly filled with clangs of metal. The cardinals circled warily, looking for the blue jays' weak positions. The blue jays were cautious too, and whenever they sensed that the cardinals were aiming at a particular place, they sent more birds to fight there.

At first the blue jays' defenses seemed to be holding. But then a lean cardinal managed to slip through into the food store and back out again, unnoticed by others. He had a bag in his claw. Stolen food! Skylion spotted him. With a roar he charged upon the cardinal, and the cardinal waved his sword in response. They parried each other's moves, their figures almost lost in the whirl of silver that was their blades. Finally, Skylion sliced the rope around the neck of the bag, and the sack dropped into the grass below. Relieved of his heavy burden so suddenly, the cardinal lost his balance. For a moment his defenses were down and his neck was exposed.

Instinctively, Skylion raised his sword. Yet something in him stirred. . . . The noises around him faded away into silence. *Peace is more important, Skylion.* Glenagh's voice haunted him, and he could almost see the elder shaking his head disapprovingly. The blue jay leader felt weak and unsure. He couldn't—just couldn't—bring down his sword upon the young cardinal. The cardinal closed his eyes and tensed his neck, waiting for the blue jay's blow. . . .

The noises of the battle returned. Skylion quickly shifted the angle of his blow so that the flat of the blade thumped on the cardinal's shoulder.

The cardinal opened his eyes and locked them for a second with Skylion's. There was surprise in his eyes, and perhaps some gratitude. Then he was gone, disappearing behind the other battling birds.

The blue jays held out stubbornly. Fighters from both sides were getting tired. The blue jays were light and agile in build, while the cardinals were muscular and heavy-framed. Slowly, very slowly, the blue jays drove the cardinals back toward the Line.

There the cardinals decided to hold their ground and retreat no more. The battle would be decided on the tallest mound of the Appleby Hills. One minute the blue jays seemed to be winning, but the cardinals gained advantage in the next. The red mingled with the blue, fighting, beating, and yelling at one another.

Shadow, Turnatt's scout, hid in a tall tree nearby, smiling cruelly at the fighting cardinals and blue jays. "It's better than I thought!" he crackled. "Wait until His Majesty hears about this!"

Aska had left the Bluewingle camp quietly that morning, before the attack by the cardinals. She was a pretty blue jay, with glossy feathers, a sweet voice, a

graceful figure, and eyes that were like deep pools of dark chocolate. She sighed. The whole thing was too confusing for her to understand and to accept. The fights and battles. *How did the cardinals ever become our enemies? We were good friends a month ago. Why not now?* She missed seeing her best cardinal friends. She missed playing on the Appleby Hills, where the sun shone brightly and dandelions carpeted the ground, making the hills golden as far as the eye could see. It was now cardinal territory, and the blue jays stayed away. She missed the taste of the cardinals' special raspberry pies with golden, honey-covered crusts and sweet, sticky fillings.

The more Aska thought, the dizzier she became. Sitting alone on a quiet branch did not help. She looked around. A small creek gurgled peacefully nearby, and the fragrance of the early spring flowers drifted to her nostrils. The scene would normally make Aska happy, but not now.

The blue jay, catching an uplift, rose unsteadily into the air. Thoughts whirled in her head as she flew in the direction she thought was toward home. She shut her eyes for a second to clear her thoughts. When she opened them, she found herself staring at shadows that floated in the air. The shadows moved toward her.

Flea-screech grumbled unhappily. He hadn't eaten a proper meal for four days. He and five soldiers had been sent out to capture woodbirds, but they had found nothing. He knew he would be punished if he came back with nothing more than half-starved soldiers.

Living on thin acorn soup and dandelion roots was not the kind of life Flea-screech wanted. In despair he kicked the mossy ground. By chance a wad of moss hit another crow on his beak, muffling his surprised gurgle. Flea-screech stared angrily at the soldier, and the soldier stared back, each thinking of his own misery.

Flea-screech's thoughts were interrupted by an excited whisper: "Sir, there's a blue jay flying not far from here who could be easily surrounded and captured!"

Seconds later, the crows flew off toward the flying blue speck. It wouldn't know what the shadows were until it was too late.

"Help!" Aska screamed as she realized what was happening. Darting this way and that, she flew in complex patterns and then sped away, careless of her direction. The crows tried to surround her. She knew that they were bigger and heavier than she was, so she flew her fastest through thick, mazelike groves and bushes. The crashes and yells of pain told her that her plan was working. But the crows kept following.

Fueled by her fright, she flew even faster. There were at least three birds behind her, or possibly even five. Aska shuddered at the thought. The dense bushes wouldn't last forever, she knew. They ended only ten feet away. As she burst out into open air, another crow tried to block her path. She yelped in surprise and, seeing no other way to avoid a collision, zoomed under the bird. The dumbfounded crow shrieked with rage.

"Oh, you sly blue jay!" Aska heard the crow cry. "Soldiers!" he yelled over the loud whooshing of their wings. "Chase that blue jay south toward Fortress Glooming! We'll have it cornered!"

Aska flew through strange and murky territories, neither blue jays' nor cardinals'. She peered about for good places to hide. Her wings were getting sore from the flight. *Oh, somebird help me!* she thought, taking no notice of the rain that bounced off her shoulders and dampened her feathers.

"You tricky blue jay! I'll get you, me and my crew will!" The voices pursuing Aska were getting louder as the crows drew closer. After ducking under a bush and hearing the crows crash into it, Aska saw a startling scene, a half-built fortress towering over a great stretch of young birches and cedars, the height of a typical old pine tree. As her eyes swept down, she saw stone blocks piled on the ground, waiting to be used to build another wall. Through the rain she could make out a small patch of tall grass just beyond them. Gathering all her strength, she darted between the grass stalks, breathing hard. She heard the loud whoosh as her pursuers whizzed past, still yelling and howling.

Aska's feathers were damp, too damp for her to lift her wings and fly without difficulty. Her breath came in short gasps. The rain made a rhythmic sound on the grass leaves above her head. What was she going to do now?

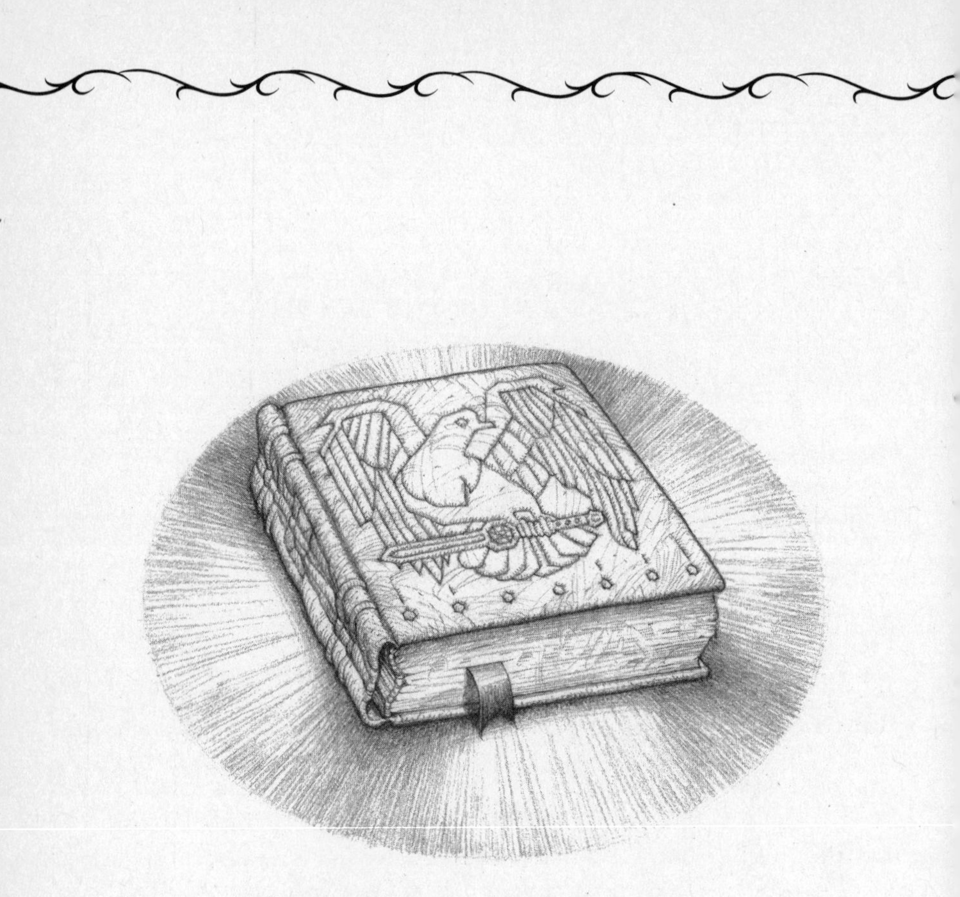

The road to success is full of thorns.

—FROM THE *OLD SCRIPTURE*

5
THE WOODBIRD IN THE GRASS

Just as Aska encountered Flea-screech and his soldiers, the slavebirds were given a little break because rain threatened to fall. No soldier wanted to get wet standing guard as the slaves worked.

Tilosses poked his head through the wooden bars of the slave compound and glanced at the gray sky. Quickly ducking in as a cold wind chilled him, the old sparrow sighed. Would the rain keep Miltin from carrying out his plan?

Tilosses quickly looked up, beckoning Miltin over with a nod. The old sparrow told the robin all he had heard while eavesdropping on Turnatt's conversations with Slime-beak and the scout, Shadow.

"They are going to kill us when the fortress is finished," Miltin whispered to himself. He thanked Tilosses for telling him the news and then fell silent, deep in thought.

The slaves waited anxiously, having small and pointless conversations. Rain beat down on the wooden roof of the slave compound, making a dull rhythm as well as many bothersome drips that created wet spots on the dirty floor. *Plip, plop, plip, plop.* The wet spots became muddy puddles and finally small pools of brown water. The birds paid no mind. The rich smell of earth and worn wood filled the air. Miltin sat huddled in a corner with rags for blankets. He lowered his gaze and studied a pool of water intently. The puddle rippled every time a drop of water fell into it. *Soon most of us will be killed,* he thought. *Many of the woodbirds in the forest will be captured by cruel Turnatt, just like the big mud puddle swallowing the small drops of the water from the roof. No! We can't wait passively to be killed; we can't allow new birds to be tortured and pinioned. . . . The woodbirds can't be captured! They are our only chance!* He jumped up.

"I'm going to ask Slime-beak for permission to gather wood now," he said in a calm voice. He scanned all the birds in the crowd. Glipper gave him a wing tip–up. Tilosses nodded. The rest of the birds were looking at him. As unruffled as possible, Miltin spun on his heel and marched out of the slave compound.

"Wow, I don't know how he'll do it, but he's taking some risk," a slavebird commented. "If he's caught talking to a native woodbird . . ."

Tilosses was anxious too. He wished luck to the robin with a worried smile.

The rain was beating down harder than ever, creating a foglike curtain that concealed nearly everything. Turnatt growled unhappily, staring at the window and glancing at the door. The rain had halted work on the fortress. It made everything damp and forlorn. Turnatt nibbled at a roasted salmon that had gone cold within minutes. He washed the unappetizing meat down with white grape wine. *The hateful rain!* Anger boiled up in the hawk lord. He looked around, disgusted, and tightened his grip on the salmon carcass. The hawk growled again. He tossed the fish at the door just as it opened creakily. The salmon missed its target and hit Slime-beak full on the beak with a loud smack, causing him to stumble. Turnatt whipped his head around, his eye glaring. Slime-beak realized as he peeled the fish from his face that this wasn't a good moment to talk to the hawk lord. But as he brushed sticky scales from his feathers, he knew that he couldn't simply walk away. He was trapped.

Turnatt let out a deafening yell of rage. All of his feathers stood up on end, making him look larger and more terrifying. Slime-beak shuddered slightly. He began to edge back through the door.

"What business do you have here, you rubbish of a crow?" Turnatt thundered. "To make trouble, eh? I'll send you to the torture rack before sunset. That will teach you who's in charge!" The mere mention of the rack chilled Slime-beak's blood. He stared helplessly at the ground.

"W-w-what did I do wrong, milord?" the crow captain squeaked out as he nervously twiddled with a piece of salmon tangled in his neck feathers. "I told Bug-eye to put the slavebirds on half rations and double work, made the soldiers run five laps every morning, and had them pay tribute to you as you told me to, milord. I made sure the old slavebird on kitchen duty wasn't up to anything and I—"

Turnatt scowled. "Silence, crow!" he boomed. The whole place shook with the impact of the piercing voice, and the crow captain stopped picking at the fish, only to whimper in fright. His small, beady eyes were darting around nervously. Turnatt continued: "I hear that you and your birds have been slacking too much. The soldiers are too lazy and fat! And now you're planning to let a slave outside to gather firewood. Have you ordered a soldier as an overseer?"

"N-no, milord . . . but he has t-to check with me before he g-goes, milord—"

"Oh, you crow! Haven't you got any brains?"

"Milord! Even if he escapes, it's just one slavebird!"

"No, no. I don't think you've got any brains at all! What if the slave finds the native woodbirds? My plans will be ruined. Ruined! To think that you are a captain! Why, crow, you're not even fit for a soldier. Find that slave! Go out in the rain and be his overseer! One more false move and you'll feel the consequences of such actions, worthless crow!" The words were nearly enough to make Slime-beak faint from dread. But he was too frightened to fall.

Lord Turnatt stared down at the crow captain. His eye narrowed into a glowing golden slit that hypnotized the crow. "Well?" the hawk demanded. "Get!" All of a sudden

Slime-beak felt his feet again. With an unexpected burst of energy, the crow dashed off on wobbly legs, stumbling twice, with the hawk's voice still ringing in his ears.

"Go and find that slave, you crow!"

Slime-beak dashed into the slave compound to find Miltin. The startled birds inside quickly stood at attention as the nervous captain paced from one wooden wall to the other, searching for the face of the robin slavebird who had asked him for the job of getting firewood. *No, it can't be!* The bird was nowhere to be found.

"What are you gaping at? Go back to what you were doing!" Slime-beak shouted as he dashed off. Tripping and yelling, he made toward the fortress's gate.

Miltin hopped rapidly toward the gate of the fortress. He ventured over rapid streams of muddy rainwater, slid over slippery, smooth rocks, and vaulted over large, moss-covered sticks as quickly as he could. Miltin squinted blurrily at the fortress gate before him as rain trickled down his neck and shoulders and onto his tail. Twice he slipped and fell, but that only made his pace quicker.

He had reached the farthest his chains would allow him when Slime-beak almost ran into him.

The captain glared. "What? Hide-and-seek? I gave

you permission to gather wood, not to wander hither and thither. And why do you want to go out and get wood in this weather?"

"Sir! Captain, sir! We've run out of wood, sir, and if I don't gather any more, we'll perish with cold and fever and be unable to work, sir!" Miltin answered.

Slime-beak growled, "Fine, fine, as long as you don't catch fever yourself and pass it on to the others." The captain detached Miltin's chain from the wall and secured it to his claw. He opened the gate with a key and pushed the slavebird out. "Now go! Get the firewood!"

Miltin obediently started out into the rain, with Slime-beak trailing behind, muttering curses about the bad weather.

Miltin and Slime-beak gradually reached the fringe of the forest and the shadows under the tall pines. Miltin felt a little troubled. *How can anybird be out in the rain? And even if I find them, with that captain right behind me . . .* He glanced back at Slime-beak's tired, sour face. *I have to try.*

With a cautious air the robin used his claws and beak to lash together the driest wood he could find with grass stalks. He pretended to be deeply absorbed in his task. Down came his head, his eyes glued on the wood. Up came his tail, twitching as he decided which piece was the driest. He peeked at his surroundings now and then and started, very slowly, to go farther and farther away from Slime-beak. Miltin carved every detail and landmark into his memory. Farther, farther away . . . The robin worked his way toward a small creek edged with clumps of tall grass. . . . Farther, farther . . .

"Robin slave! Where do you think you're going?" came the angry rasp.

Miltin thought fast. "Oh! I think I heard the hunting cry of a falcon! Help!"

"What? From where?"

Miltin put on a show with frantic hops and gestures. "There! There! It's closer! Can't you hear it?"

When the confused captain turned around, Miltin dived into the tall grasses and crawled silently out of sight. His intention was to investigate something—something blue, barely visible between the stalks.

"Hey! Hey, slave! Where are you lurking? Trying to escape?" The cry of Slime-beak was faint in the distance.

The noise of rustling was surprising. Aska looked around. "W-w-who's there?" she asked in a trembling voice. She saw a long, sharp stick lying on the damp ground below and quickly grabbed it and pointed it in the direction of the noise. "Who are you, and what are you doing there?" she demanded. The noise stopped.

"Shhhhhh!" Out from the shadows a robin appeared. Judging from his expression, Aska knew that the bird was almost as surprised as she was. There was no greed or evil in his eyes, and he carried no weapons. He certainly bore no resemblance to the birds that had chased her. She decided this bird was friendly.

Miltin lowered his voice. "I'm called Miltin, a slave-bird from Fortress Glooming. You are native to here, I suppose?"

"Aye."

"Then you're the bird I'm looking for."

"Why?"

"We slavebirds urgently need the local birds' help to wipe out a hawk, Turnatt. The tyrant moved here a month ago and also wants your tribes to be slaves for him. He ordered his soldiers to cause trouble by stealing eggs and food from you and the cardinals."

"Slavebird wood gatherer! Come out!" Slime-beak's voice could be heard in the distance.

"Turnatt has more than a hundred soldiers. Please ask your tribe to help us, for our sake and your own. Remember what I said. And your name?"

"Aska, of the Bluewingle tribe. Which way's north?"

Miltin quickly nodded and pointed to the right direction.

Aska darted away in a flash, hardly making any noise. Miltin heard the faint sound of "good-bye," all that was left of the blue jay.

Miltin no longer feared the captain who wielded whips or the tyrant whose yell seemed like thunder. He'd done what he had planned to do. After speedily gathering chunks of wood and lashing them together with grass stalks, he stepped out of the grass.

"Well!" Slime-beak demanded. "What were you

doing? There was no falcon you needed to hide from, so why did you go disappearing?"

"Sir! I thought the falcon had landed, and I was afraid, sir."

"Oh! Never mind. Go back to the compound right away!" ordered the captain.

"Yes, sir!"

Slime-beak followed the slavebird, with a sigh of relief.

When we are in the dark,
a shout may make us alert.
—FROM THE *OLD SCRIPTURE*

6
ASKA'S WORDS

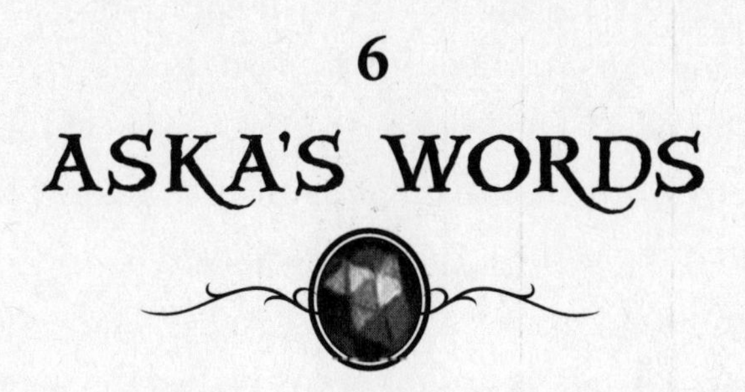

The rain drenched the red and the blue. Despite that, they still fought, wing against wing, claw against claw, sword against sword. They mingled and then separated. They all fought for one thing: to stop the thieving. They fought yelling; they fought crying. They were desperate.

Aska passed the Line. She saw her tribe's fighters and the cardinals battling one another. She closed her eyes and breathed in heavily as feelings of anger, despair, sadness, and eagerness exploded from her heart. *I must stop them and let them know the truth!* she thought, claws clenched tight. Rainwater rushed down, hard and fast. Aska did not mind. She tipped her head back as she let the words thunder from her throat. "Why do you fight? Stop! We have been fooled by a ruthless hawk who entered Stone-Run not long ago. It is the hawk who stole our eggs and food. His fortress is not far away; realize the danger. We shouldn't be fighting; be friends. Let peace and friendship be among us again. *Stop!*"

The call from Aska echoed in the forest. The rain roared in reply, the wind howled, and the trees shook.

The birds stopped battling. Aska panted as she looked from tribe to tribe. Her eyes begged them to believe her.

"Do you think she is telling the truth?"

"What if she is?"

"How can we know?"

Birds whispered among themselves. Skylion and Flame-back signaled to their warriors. They backed off.

The fighters from both tribes still gripped their weapons tightly in case the signal for attack came again. Each eyed the other side warily.

"Get the wounded back to our camp," Skylion said all of a sudden. "Then we'll hear what Aska has to say."

Seeing the blue jays retreat from the Line, the cardinals did the same. Able-bodied birds helped their wounded comrades to fly.

It was raining harder. Water and blood—the Line's ground was soaked with them. A raven flew above: an amber-eyed raven. He cawed with displeasure as he passed, disappearing into the distance.

"Oh, Skylion!" Glenagh exclaimed when he heard what had happened at the Line. He shook his head sadly and was silent. Skylion sighed deeply.

"I know. But at that moment it just seemed so . . . well, the right thing to do. I shouldn't have done it. Then things would be different—" The blue jay leader preened his blue wing. He looked up. "Oh . . . it's just . . ." He looked down again.

"Here. Have a tea cake, Skylion. Regretting things that have already happened doesn't help. Everybird makes mistakes. Though this is a big one, I think you did what you thought was right and good for your tribe, and that's what really matters. You cared about your tribe."

Skylion accepted the pastry. "Aska told us that it's a hawk who caused this rift between the cardinals and us. Now the hawk wants to catch us as slaves to build his fortress."

"So to unite with the cardinals is at the top of our list now, thank Swordbird," Glenagh said a bit more cheerfully, and poured himself a cup of tea.

Skylion nodded. "If they believe us," he said. "If they're willing to forgive what we've done."

Glenagh took a sip out of his teacup before replying. "I'm sure they will, somehow. I do hope I'll see that Flame-back again, and Fleet-tail. Smart birds, you know." He paused a moment. "Shall we talk to Aska now, Skylion? I would certainly like to hear her full story."

Fleet-tail tested his injured wing. It hurt only a little bit now, but he was still unable to fly. He looked up from the soft grass bedding he was resting on. "Flame-back, it's not your fault, you know."

The cardinal leader was in a somber state of mind. "Oh, Fleet-tail, you just said that for the millionth time to make me feel better. But it is! The whole thing is! I started to steal from the blue jays after I saw them taking our food and flying away."

Fleet-tail shook his head. His eyes glittered. "You know, if Aska was telling the truth, then it wasn't the blue jays after all."

Flame-back thought about what his friend had said as

he nibbled on a piece of dried fruit. "You might be right. I wish things were like the past. But how do we know Aska was telling the truth?" He paused. "Not to change the subject, but are the other injured all right?"

Fleet-tail scoffed. "Better off than I am, certainly. They healed quickly. All of them can fly now except me . . . poor me, you know."

Flame-back managed a smile. "But your wounds will heal soon, my friend, and then there might—just might—be peace."

Later that night Flame-back perched on his resting branch, wondering. *Maybe Aska was speaking the truth; maybe she was telling a lie.* How could he be sure? What should he do? Flame-back sighed and tucked his head under his wing. He drifted to sleep in a troubled state of mind.

In his dream the cardinal leader saw a huge fortress—with slavebirds, soldiers, and all. A large brownish red hawk strutted around, barking orders. Suddenly Flame-back was in the air, overlooking the half-finished building. Much to his surprise, the place was not far from his home. *A fortress in the Stone-Run Forest?*

Yes, a voice said. *A fortress right in the Stone-Run Forest, not far from your camp and the blue jays'.*

Flame-back's heart skipped a beat.

Yes, Aska was telling the truth, the loud, magnificent voice repeated.

"Wh-who are you?" the cardinal leader asked in a shaking voice. The clouds shimmered with a silver radiance, making the cardinal squint. Inside Flame-back could make out the shape of an awe-inspiring white bird. His wingspan was many times the cardinal leader's, stretching for yards.

The glorious bird spoke. *Ahhh, Flame-back . . . my given name is Wind-voice.* The bird smiled.

"Swordbird!" gasped the cardinal leader. He immediately bowed his head.

No need for that, red one.

Flame-back looked up. He could now see the sword of the bird glistening and the Leasorn gem reflecting the sliver of light. He shook his crested head slightly. "Swordbird, if Aska's words are true, what should I do?"

Peace, said the voice. *Now back to your dwelling, Flame-back. I have shown you what was to be shown.*

The next thing Flame-back knew, he was back home.

That was a strange dream, he thought. *But I think it's true. . . .*

You are right, it is. Remember, Flame-back, peace. The magnificent voice echoed in the cardinal's head.

Flame-back smiled faintly. "Thanks, Swordbird," he whispered as he nestled his head into his feathers again.

The blue jays perched in a circle, listening to Aska's tale.

"And that's why we fought, I think. It seems only logical," said Aska with a sigh.

"This is outrageous," fumed Cody, one of the blue jay warriors. "A fortress governed by a rotten hawk right here in Stone-Run without our knowing it?"

Aska nodded. "He turned us against the cardinals, but we had no idea."

"Aska said Turnatt has a hundred-odd soldiers," Skylion said. "We are greatly outnumbered. We couldn't force them out of here, even if each and every one of us were brave and skillful in battle." The blue jays remained quiet for a while.

"We need to prepare in case the hawk Turnatt ever comes to attack and capture us," said Glenagh. "Looks like we'll have to team up with the cardinals."

"And be friends with them again," added Brontë, another warrior.

Cody tensed. "But what if they think we are attacking them? They may not trust us after all that's happened. . . ." There were murmurs in the crowd as each bird expressed his own opinion.

"We'll have to take the risk," said Aska with a determined tone in her voice. "We need to." Other voices agreed.

"It's worth a try," Skylion said.

The next day a party of blue jays, bearing no weapons, flew toward the Line with light hearts. They all hoped that soon the Line wouldn't exist anymore. Memories of the past filled them. Happy for the first time in weeks, they veered into cardinal territory. Even the sun seemed to be shining brighter. They soared through the air, over the Silver Creek and the Appleby

Hills. But they still felt a bit nervous when they saw the Cardinals' camp. There they perched on various trees but did not surround the camp.

"Flame-back, my friend!" Skylion called in a voice full of kindness, the voice he had used before the conflict between the two tribes. "It is I, Skylion, and the Bluewingles."

Soon Flame-back appeared, calm and solemn. A slight hint of surprise flickered in the cardinal leader's eyes.

"Skylion?" he said. "Skylion?" There was a long pause.

Then all of the Sunrise army appeared. They didn't have any weapons either. The two tribes just stood, facing each other in silence.

"Come inside, my friends," Flame-back whispered. "Come inside."

"Theater? What's a theater?" I felt silly asking such a question. The old bird winked at me cheerfully. "Oh . . . a delightful package of music and fun, wrapped in all sorts of colors, if you know what I mean." Unfortunately, I did not.

—FROM EWINGERALE'S DIARY IN THE *OLD SCRIPTURE*

7

The Flying Willowleaf Theater

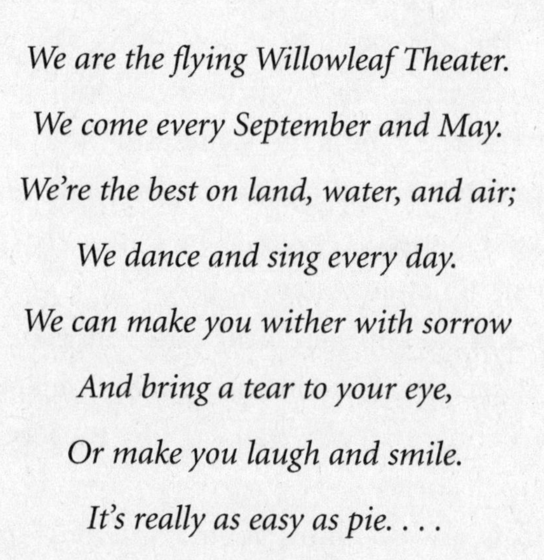

We are the flying Willowleaf Theater.

We come every September and May.

We're the best on land, water, and air;

We dance and sing every day.

We can make you wither with sorrow

And bring a tear to your eye,

Or make you laugh and smile.

It's really as easy as pie. . . .

The carefree song rang in the marshes of the Peridot River, along with laughter and the silky notes of the harmonica. The Willowleaf Theater birds perched in the basket of their hot-air balloon, singing and playing with all their might.

"Well, here we are, on to Stone-Run again," said Kastin, a titmouse, as the last notes faded away into the marshes and forests below.

Parrale, the wood duck, nodded slowly as she unpacked a map. "I wonder what the blue jays and the cardinals are up to this year. They always have surprises."

"Where shall we perform this year? I like the Appleby Hills. There's nothing like them!" Mayflower, the junco, exclaimed. She peered over the basket and looked longingly in the direction of Stone-Run. The snakelike Peridot River led to the flying theater's destination.

"Don't forget the food—chestnut and watercress stews, mushroom and onion patties fried with cinnamon, beetle salads, raspberry pies, strawberry shortcakes, fresh honey atop soft nut bread . . . oh . . . and there are drinks of all kinds, all delicious!" the gannet Lorpil added cheerfully, his button eyes glittering at the thought. Parrale shot him a look. Dilby, the loon, tittered and shook his head.

"Food is all you think about," the loon teased. He

added more coal to the burner. The hot-air balloon rose higher into the sky. "I personally like how eager they are to hear the stories of Swordbird. They love our plays about when he appeared and helped the desperate, about his courageous battles for peace, and about his sword, with its Leasorn gem. You know, on the earth there are only seven other Leasorn gems."

Lorpil tried to stifle a yawn as he steadied himself against the edge of the basket. "*Mm-hmm* . . . History, history, history . . . very interesting."

Mayflower took a small picture of Swordbird from her pocket. "Lorpil! How dare you! Swordbird's stories are my favorite too."

"Well, I know my role well enough in our Swordbird play," Lorpil said. "So I'm flying ahead a bit." He took off from the edge of the basket, which tipped and swayed dangerously. Parrale looked cross.

"In the name of Swordbird, Lorpil! For the twentieth time, be careful with the takeoff!"

"What a wacko, that gannet," said Kastin. Alexandra, the hummingbird, agreed.

"He drives me bananas," complained Dilby.

Lorpil's voice was heard in the distance. "Bananas? Did somebird say bananas? Save one for me. I love them, especially sliced ones fried in olive oil, but plain ones are yummy too. . . ."

Parrale let out a sigh. "Oh well. Let's practice one more song."

Lorpil scanned the sky, trying to find a suitable place for a rest, a bath, and a meal. Because of his passion for acting, he had left his beloved seaside to join the Willowleaf Theater. Almost any chance he got, he would fly down to a nice, calm stream or pool to rest, swim, and eat some water greens and find some river snails.

Gliding over with the updraft, he followed the course of the Peridot River. After the second curve he discovered it: a nice, sandy shore shaded by weeping willows. Lorpil greeted the sight with a pleased gannet cry. He flew in smaller circles now and dived down with a small splash. After snacking on different types of water plants and prying a few mussels off their rocks, the gannet came ashore and rested in the sunlight. There was a whisper of wings brushing against leaves.

"Shadow . . . keep it down . . . the woodbirds are still unaware . . . what . . ."

"Stop it, pumpkin brain . . . can't you see . . . blue jays . . . cardinals . . . slavebirds . . . good idea, eh?"

Lorpil spun around, his eyes darting this way and that, feathers bristling, wings ready for takeoff. There was nothing except a few dark shadows disappearing almost without noise. Lorpil blinked in surprise. *What's wrong? Why were those birds so secretive and talking about things like "slavebirds" and "unaware"?*

Lorpil tried to make sense of everything, but soon he gave up and resumed slurping on the mussels. There were so many things that the gannet didn't understand; he didn't bother to ponder them all. Still, he was glad that his feathers blended into the white sand so he hadn't been seen. He took off as quietly as possible, heading toward the green and white hot-air balloon.

O joy be on the day of the Bright Moon Festival!
Holy day of Swordbird's birth,
a day when birds sing and dance,
and when a round,
bright moon shines onto the earth.
—FROM THE *OLD SCRIPTURE*

8
The Bright Moon Festival

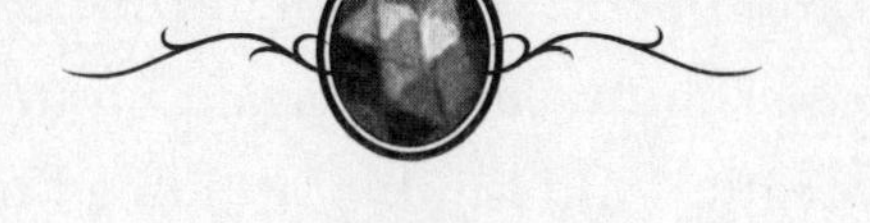

The Bright Moon Festival, which was held under the first full moon of spring, was a day of celebration of the birth of Swordbird. The red and the blue had always celebrated this event on the tallest mount of the Appleby Hills, because the view of the moon from there was the best. No clouds dared to rest above it on the blessed night.

The Willowleaf Theater troupe arrived just as the sky

darkened. They were greeted with great applause and excited cries. The stage was soon set, the props were in place, and the show began.

"Ladies and gentlebirds, introducing the flying Willowleaf Theater!" Dilby smiled broadly. "First, an acrobatic juggling show. The more hoops, the better, and more trouble if the hoops fall!" Dilby backed out from the stage.

The curtains opened with a high-pitched squeak.

"Need to oil those curtains again," muttered Parrale under her breath. "And think of it, I oiled them just last week!"

Alexandra the hummingbird darted onstage. Dilby appeared playfully twirling three red, yellow, and blue hoops.

The hummingbird swung around in rhythmic circles, flying through the hoops with amazing poise and speed.

"Faster, faster, faster we go!" chanted Dilby.

Soon the fun made everybird chant, "*Faster, faster, faster we go!*" The blue jays and the cardinals in the crowd bobbed their heads to the rhythm, while Dilby, muttered, "Oh no . . . oh no . . . I'm going to drop them," and juggled the colorful hoops without missing a beat. Alexandra kept up with the hoops, doing flips and twirls and flying upside down.

The curtains creakily closed with a final note from the music. Deafening applause followed, along with the yells "Bravo!" "Go, Allie!" and "Magnificent juggling, Dilby!"

Dilby returned to the stage for the second time. His feathers were damp with sweat, and his breath was a little heavy.

"Next, a Swordbird play, to honor our guardian of peace!" He bowed and backed away.

Parrale walked slowly to the stage, matching her steps to the sad music. When the wood duck reached the center, she stopped and slowly turned to the audience.

Mournfully she sang in a deep voice:

The sun's rays have dried the earth;
Every drop of water is gone.
Dust and death are everywhere.
No longer fair is the dawn!

Kastin and Mayflower came from the right, singing softly in chorus, "Dust and death, destruction and doom, now is a time of darkness. . . ."

They bowed their heads, and the audience listened to the sorrowful melody in the background.

Suddenly a high, sweet voice sang out. "Yet there is

Swordbird, there is Swordbird. He will help us all." And Alexandra appeared from the left.

Backstage, a violinist played a hopeful tune. All four birds brightened and sang in harmony:

Swordbird! Swordbird!
Please use your magic sword to make us rain!
Swordbird, Swordbird, let our days
be filled with joy again!

Dilby laid down his violin. "It's time, Lorpil," he said. They both strapped belts (which were connected to a gigantic kite) around their waists and across their shoulders.

"Ready?" Lorpil put on a backpack and picked up a long wooden pole that was fashioned into a large sword.

Dilby intently listened for the signal notes. "Go!"

The two took off, bursting from backstage and out into view of the audience. They flew high, flapping their wings hard. As they gained speed, the white kite unfurled into shape above them, becoming a giant white bird. The two birds became the claws of Swordbird, and Lorpil's pole became his sword.

The red and the blue gasped and applauded.

“Swordbird!” Parrale, Mayflower, Kastin, and Alexandra all shouted.

“Swordbird!” the audience echoed.

Lorpil and Dilby hovered above the stage.

“This is my favorite part,” said Lorpil, grinning and winking at Dilby. He shouted to the night sky, “Come, rain!” and waved his sword. Dilby tore open his backpack. A silvery shower of tiny objects fell out of the bag and onto the stage and audience below.

“Rain at last! Rain at last! Thank Swordbird, there is rain at last!” the actors yelled, picking up the candied fruits and nuts in foil wrappers from the ground and tossing them up.

The cardinals and the blue jays laughed as they collected the treats and joined in the shouting. “Rain! Rain!” The play ended with all of the birds, both actors and audience, eating the candied fruits and nuts.

Dilby came up the stage again. “Now is the moment everybird is waiting for: good food between acts and a break for our tiring actors, eh?” Laughter echoed over the Appleby Hills.

Soon the tables were buzzing with merry talk and filled with food of all kinds, the last of the winter store. There was not quite as much as there had been in other years; Turnatt’s thieving had taken its toll. Still, everybird found a favorite treat somewhere on the long wooden tables.

"Pass the cream, please."

"*Mmm* . . . try this raspberry pie, Brontë. It's great! I've missed it; we haven't had enough berries to make any after the hawk's thievery. Good thing your tribe did!"

"Hey, little one, aren't you going to try some Stone-Run stew?"

"But I need to finish eating these grilled caterpillars first!"

"Hey! Who ate all the potato salad?"

"Don't hog up the food, Lorpil!"

"Best beetles I've tasted in quite a while . . . crunchy and delicious!"

It had been many dawns and sunsets since the laughter of the red and the blue rang sweet and clear in Stone-Run Forest. Now the trees seemed to listen quietly to the birds and rejoice along with them.

Back at Fortress Glooming, Turnatt had decided that it was time to attack the cardinals and the bluejays. The current slavebirds were like leaves trembling in the late-autumn wind, so weak that work on his magnificent fortress was going slower than a snail's pace. He needed new slaves, and quickly, he thought as he sat alone in his chamber, clutching the *Book of Heresy*.

Once Turnatt had been an ordinary red hawk, no more fearsome than most of his kind. He snorted in disgust to remember it. In those days he had dwelled in makeshift burrows and had had no ambitions beyond the next meal he could catch. All of that horror had changed one day when he had taken shelter from a rainstorm in a cave, a crack in the face of a tall cliff. There, tucked away in a niche in the wall, he had found an old leather-bound book, the *Book of Heresy*.

From the first page, the first sentence, Turnatt had been bewitched. He thought about it in the daytime, dreamed about it at night, and even slept with his head resting on the musty, ancient pages of the dark tome. There was one passage in particular that he turned back to again and again. It told him that if a bird ate a woodbird egg every day, he would live for years and years—perhaps forever!

Turnatt had started to raid woodbirds' nests, but it was hard work; the little birds fought furiously to defend their young, so every egg was bought with scars and bruises. Turnatt did not want to waste his time to battle woodbirds. He found himself a band of crows and ravens and ordered them to do his nest raiding for him.

Then he'd needed servants to care for his army and somewhere for them to live. That was when he had decided to catch woodbirds as slaves and force them to build him a luxurious fortress.

The *Book of Heresy* had been his cherished companion through it all. It had transformed him from an ordinary bird in rags who lived worse than tramps to a sly tyrant in silks who dwelled better than kings! Turnatt stroked the leather cover with a gentle claw. He had sent Slime-beak out to bring back cardinals and blue jays. They'd be strong, sturdy workers. Soon his fortress would be complete. And everything that the *Book of Heresy* had promised him would come true!

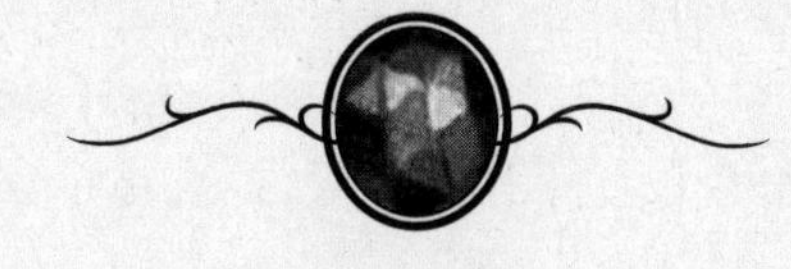

Don't forget unexpected dangers in times of peace.

—FROM THE *OLD SCRIPTURE*

9
DANGER

Slime-beak flew toward the camps of the cardinals and the blue jays, feeling quite puffed up and mighty. He, captain of Fortress Glooming, was leading a major attack. He followed the directions Shadow had given him and confidently led his band of fifty or so crows and ravens. According to Shadow, he should head for the Appleby Hills, the high spot at the center between the camps of the red and the blue. Slime-beak was enjoying himself greatly when he caught a glimpse of the hills in the distance and slowed his flight. On one of the hills were a tent, a stage, and a blur of birds fluttering about.

"Ho, soldier, those are cardinals and blue jays over there?" Slime-beak jabbed a raven with a claw.

"Aye, Captain, sir! Looks like they're having a party of some sort, sir!"

"*Hmm* . . . But how and why? Shadow assured me they were hopping mad with one another." An idea popped into the captain's head. "The plan has to change. Let's *really* surprise them. Spread out over by the woodlands, east and north. Let's not fail Lord Turnatt!" The shadowlike birds obeyed.

During the feast Parrale and some other birds had gone to fetch the glossy black piano from the hot-air balloon's basket. Though it was a miniature piano that was made especially for birds, it was still quite heavy. Many helped to move it. Tugging and pushing and pulling, they dragged it out. Finally, after great effort, the piano was in its proper place.

Parrale, sweating and huffing, said with a smile, "Yes, this is the moment everybird has been expecting: song and dance!" The cardinals and the blue jays in the crowd swallowed their last beakfuls. They cheered with cries of approval. "You choose the song, the dance, the singer, and the dancers," Parrale announced.

With a nod Kastin and Mayflower flew with a single

flap of their wings to their positions on the piano, Kastin on the high keys, Mayflower on the low. They waited.

In the crowd Brontë nudged Cody. "Come on, Cody! Go up and sing! You have the best voice for miles around!" This attracted the attention of the birds nearby, who supported Brontë.

"Listen to your friend!"

"Don't be shy!"

"Let's not delay the program!"

Cody grumbled good-naturedly. "As long as I can get rid of all those chatterers. If I go off tune, it won't be my fault."

As Cody made his way up to the stage, Flame-back came out of the audience and patted the blue jay's shoulder.

"I've missed your cheery little tunes, Cody. Sing for the Bluewingles. And for us." Then the cardinal leader slipped back into the crowd, vanishing behind other birds.

"We've got a singer!" called Lorpil. Then he turned his attention to Cody. "Just fly up to the lid of the piano, eh?"

Cody hopped to the piano lid and surveyed the crowd below. Many were watching, and most were silent.

"Shhhhhh!"

Kastin perched on a piano key. "Choose a song, Cody."

"How about 'Stone-Run and All'?"

"Good choice."

Three cardinals flew up along with Aska and two other blue jays.

"Can we dance?" Aska questioned. "It's our favorite song."

Mayflower nodded.

The six dancers took their positions: three red birds on one side, three blue on the other.

"Ready? Sing on the high C, after we play the introduction."

Kastin and Mayflower started to fly about, playing notes with their claws. The melody sounded like water, smooth and rippling.

Mayflower nodded to Cody when the last few notes rang. The blue jay took a huge breath and puffed out his chest, and the high C trembled in the air.

In the valley, there shines the sun,
On the bright forest of Stone-Run,
The rippling Peridot River,
And the Silver Creek.
This is the wonderful place that everybird seeks.

I am one . . . of Stone-Run,
Of the Bluewingle tribe, of the Sunrise.
We are one . . . of Stone-Run,
United forever.

Cody sang the first verse with a voice so touching, rich, and powerful that some birds in the audience cried.

The dancers each wore a silky scarf with the traditional Stone-Run mark—a pine tree with three birds singing in it. Graceful both in the air and on the ground, they flew in patterns, swirled and dipped their wings rhythmically, or swayed their heads to the music.

The pianists, Kastin and Mayflower, quickened their pace and played a passage in which there was no singing. If a bird listened carefully, he might hear in the music the spattering of rain or the rippling and gurgling of streams, or he might "see" the sun slowly rising on a Stone-Run morning.

The audience was so drawn into the dance and the song that they didn't pay attention to anything else. In the surroundings Slime-beak and the soldiers prepared to attack.

Surreptitious tactics are
always the best way out.
—FROM THE *BOOK OF HERESY*

10
Surprise Attack

Slime-beak surveyed the landscape where the cardinals and the blue jays were watching some kind of performance. He couldn't help feeling a little interested in the show. But a sudden vision of Lord Turnatt's angry face reminded him of his job. He glanced at the red and the blue, muttering calculations.

He scowled and spat.

"Blast my feathers! We can't outnumber them. Well,

looks like it will test our skills." The black birds silently nodded.

"Everybird, sneak up and attack them by surprise. Now."

The sky started to darken, and an owl hooted in the distance.

The cardinals and the blue jays swayed to the beat of the music. Cody, perching on the highest point of the piano, focused on a shadow to help him keep his balance. It suddenly moved, and then some black feathers appeared. Startled, Cody thought his mind was playing a trick on him. *Good thing I'm not in the middle of a verse,* Cody thought. *How embarrassing that would be!*

Shifting his focus to the dancers, he watched Aska and her friends, waiting for the high C again. After hearing it, Cody broke into song.

If you came to our tribal camps, oh, you'll see,
Many friendly birds just like me,
The cardinals and the blue jays are friends forever!
Forever . . .
The Appleby Hills bloom with flowers so sweet.
Every year at the festival, that's where we meet,

As friends, friends, friends . . .
With the—

Cody never got to finish the rest of the verse, for he spotted an army of coal-colored birds advancing. They pointed deadly, sharp arrows at the unsuspecting dancers.

"Aska! All of you dancers, duck!" he cried with a note of despair in his voice. "Move!" An arrow headed for Aska, and Cody jumped and knocked the surprised dancer to the ground. The arrow, luckily, didn't do severe damage. It just bruised Cody's shoulder.

Noise and confusion broke out in the crowd. Some tried to escape; others turned to fight the intruders. A few decided neither to fight nor to run away but to do tricks; those were the birds of the Willowleaf Theater.

At the time Dilby was still backstage, preparing for his next act, juggling with lighted torches. The loon measured distances with a careful eye and threw his torches toward thick mobs of crows and ravens. He chuckled when he heard the screams and yells.

When the arrows started to rain down, Lorpil, of course, was attacking several pies at the food table. Instantly an idea popped into his head.

"Pie their smelly faces!" he cried to the birds nearby.

"Wh-what?"

"Pie them!" Lorpil threw a large raspberry pie with all his might at one of the ravens. The pastry hit the soldier's face with a juicy squish, spattering gooey jam all over him and several nearby soldiers.

Alexandra found spoons on one of the tables. She quickly taught nine birds how to sling nuts at the enemies. The soldiers howled and squawked in surprise as the nuts hit them.

Kastin and Mayflower glanced at a gigantic container of hot soup and slowly exchanged mischievous glances. They had an idea, too.

"Here's a way to help the cardinals and the blue jays, eh, Kassie?"

"Fine by me, May. Let's tip that bean soup!"

The junco and the titmouse rushed to the steaming pot. They each grasped a handle and flew up, straining to lift the heavy container to a branch of a nearby tree. When a crowd of crows and ravens flew underneath, they tipped the hot liquid on the unsuspecting black birds. Now covered in the sticky bean soup, they plummeted and crashed to the ground.

Despite the Willowleaf Theater's efforts, Slime-beak and his soldiers kept advancing, fighting any blue jays and cardinals in the way. And soon a new threat emerged: fire arrows. Every few seconds, a volley of flaming arrows would suddenly shoot through the air, like angry snakes slithering across the coal black sky.

Some of the arrows hit the wooden panels of the stage. A few struck the balloon of the flying Willowleaf Theater. Still others of these deadly shafts ruined not only the beautiful tablecloths on the food tables but also the cakes, pies, and puddings. The air stank of burned fruit, cloth, and feathers. The red and the blue fought side by side, helping each other and trying to stop the intruders.

Slime-beak yelped as a sword dug into his shoulder. The captain spun around. The attacker was a cardinal with exceptionally large wings. The captain roared with rage, almost forgetting about his injured shoulder. No sooner had he ended his roar than a hard fight ensued. Slime-beak found himself slashing his sword with all his might to defend his life. He took cuts and bruises from the cardinal and dizzying wing clouts to his head and ears. Ducking behind another crow, Slime-beak dodged a swipe from his opponent's sword. As the cardinal was forced to face a new enemy, Slime-beak seized the chance to look around.

"Help, Captain!" screamed a nearby crow as he went down, crushed by a determined blue jay.

Many other birds of Fortress Glooming were suffering.

Slime-beak decided to check on the soldiers on the

other side of the stage. But as he came down for a landing, he slipped in a gooey, hot mess that smelled . . . like beans? A dozen of his soldiers dashed to his aid and splashed into the bean soup as well. The sticky liquid coated their feathers and glued their wings firmly to their sides. Now they could not fly.

"Oww!" Slime-beak cried sharply as a jagged piece of roasted pecan zapped him in his behind, followed by a

terrible assortment of acorns, pine nuts, chestnuts, and beechnuts bombarding his face and wings. Wincing and dancing in pain, the captain skidded between two battling birds to escape the merciless nuts that pelted his body. Just as he slipped away, another horror attacked him: a large torch flying and twirling, like a vengeful spirit. Getting out of the way, Slime-beak, bean goo and all, ran to a safe distance and watched. The torch struck an unlucky crow soldier, who yelped and immediately perished as the stink of burning feathers reached Slime-beak's nostrils. Trying to shake the blood-chilling image from his mind, the captain scrambled headfirst into a honey-covered raspberry pie, the jam filling blinding him for a sticky second. Stumbling backward, the captain received a hard, solid punch from an angry blue jay, which sent him spinning uncontrollably. "*Yah!* Away with you. Stone-Run can't be conquered!" the blue jay yelled.

The frightened captain lost his wits. He shoved everybird out of his way and turned around.

"*Ahhh!*"

"Captain Slime-beak! Help!"

"*Ow! Ow!* I'm going to die!"

"Get me back to Fortress Glooming!"

The cries of his soldiers rang in the captain's raspberry

jam–filled ears. Running as fast as he could, he trailed raspberry jam, soup, and fragments of nuts. He tripped into other soldiers as messy as he was, but nothing kept him from racing to someplace safer. Slime-beak cried out as chunks of piecrust fell from his face and into his beak.

"Retreat! Troops, back to Fortress Glooming!"

A woodbird egg a day will keep death away.

—FROM THE *BOOK OF HERESY*

11
IDEAS

That evening, as Slime-beak led a third of Turnatt's army to fight the red and the blue, the slaves at Fortress Glooming were discussing the event. It was an early-evening gathering rather than the usual campfire discussion. Tilosses had been eavesdropping lately not only on Turnatt but also on the soldiers at dinner and the cook, Bone-squawk. The old slavebird had picked up a lot of information, enough to give the slavebirds a new idea for escaping.

"How to start, my dear friends?" Tilosses began excitedly. "Escaping now could be a reality! According to what I've learned from Turnip—no, Turnatt—the cook, Bone-squawk, plus some other empty-headed soldiers from the army, I think that today, yes, today, we'll have the perfect chance to escape. We can no longer wait for the native woodbirds to come and help us; time is running out. So think about it: One third of the army is gone, Slime-beak with them. What could be better?" The slavebirds murmured among themselves, some agreeing, others doubting. "To add to that, Turnatt caught a bit of a cold and Bug-eye hurt his right claw. Swordbird made it happen all by coincidence today!"

One of the slavebirds patiently waited for the whisperings to die down. He asked the question that was on everybird's mind: "Tilosses, what is your plan?"

The old sparrow guffawed, his belly shaking a bit and his eyes glittering. "It's probably the best a bird could think up, of course." His face became stern. "Listen closely. Around midnight the guards at our compound will switch shifts. Glipper is the closest to the door, so when the new guard comes, kill him!" The sparrow handed the flycatcher some small pointed darts that were made of sticks they had secretly collected and sharpened on stones. "Next, we'll saw off our chains with this knife I stole from the kitchen. Once we're loose, we'll tipclaw around the compound and crawl behind those piles of rocks and dirt. There's a bendy old willow at the end of the rocks. We'll flutter up to the roof of the hut where Bone-squawk stores food. It's a safe place, since the hut's overshadowed by a couple of trees. After that, Miltin, Glipper, and the two vireo brothers will tackle the gate guards so they can't prevent our escape. The rest of my plan you probably can guess: Once the gate is open, we'll slide down the roof and leave Fortress Glooming."

"That's a little too risky, isn't it, Tilosses? What if the guards at the gate give the alarm?" questioned a waxwing.

Tilosses smiled. "By great fortune, tonight's guards are to be Crooked-shoulder and, what's the other's name, oh yes, Large-cap. What luck! Crooked-shoulder's eyelids always close during his shift, and Large-cap wears a cap over his eyes. That's one advantage for us.

"Add to that, Miltin on his wood-gathering mission learned that the woodbirds live north of us."

"But what if they find out that there're no birds in our

compound? Then what will we do?"

Miltin smiled craftily, his big eyes shining. "Ah. I was about to get to that point. A couple of bundles of grass here, a lump of lumber there, and dummies will do the job."

"I can almost see old Bug-eye's face when he finds the dummies." Tilosses laughed. Then he became serious. "So if everything goes well, we'll escape. In the morning it will be too late for the soldiers to find us."

"So," concluded Glipper, "let's hope all will be as smooth as cream."

In the topmost chamber of Fortress Glooming, Turnatt sat on his throne as usual. During the past few days he had caught a cold. It wasn't a serious one, but it limited his outbursts. The dizziness in the hawk's head made him dreamy and slow in thought. But at times he could still snap at his captain and soldiers, to discourage any thoughts or plans against him.

Bone-squawk, the cook, scurried into the room, carrying a blue jay egg and a cardinal one in a silver tray. The eggs stolen from the red and the blue were carefully sorted by Turnatt himself, who tapped them gently with a spoon to test their quality. Turnatt wearily inspected one egg and then the other. He chose the blue jay egg and gestured to Bone-squawk. He had eaten a cardinal egg the day before and wanted to have a different taste. The cook stepped forward, carrying a long, sharp needlelike knife. Turnatt grunted as he pointed to a spot. In went the knife, with a small crack. After Bone-squawk withdrew his tool, a good-sized hole appeared, neat and clean, with just a bit of egg white dripping out. The cook, after fumbling in his ingredients bag, poked lemon juice, onion powder, parsley, and a bit of pepper into the egg. He carefully inserted a small spoon through the hole, slowly stirring without disturbing the eggshell. Turnatt watched drowsily. Bone-squawk, with a final bow, backed out of the hawk lord's room. After a long time Turnatt finally put his beak into the hole of the egg and slowly, slowly sipped with his eye half closed.

The hawk lord was getting sleepy. He drained the egg with a final slurp, licking his beak unhurriedly. Turnatt wished his cold would go away. Little by little he drifted off with his head against the empty eggshell. He dreamed about the past.

IT WAS NOT SO LONG AGO, when he had first made plans to build a fortress, a place to house his army and to store the

stolen eggs. He would need many new slavebirds, he knew.

After taking rolled-up maps from his bookshelves and stretching them out, he hunted for a tribe that would be his next target. Far and wide on the maps he searched. At last he found an ideal tribe, the Waterthorn, near the Rockwell River. Robins were the birds there! They would certainly make good, hardy workers.

That night Turnatt started planning his attack.

The next morning he set out for the Rockwell River with fifty crows flying behind his left wing, and fifty ravens behind his right. Half a mile from the destination they split up into two groups. Some birds would attack directly as a decoy to draw out the warriors of the tribe. The rest of his horde would then take over the tribe trees, taking the birds left behind for slaves.

At first all worked according to Turnatt's plan. To Turnatt's delight, there were a lot of able-bodied birds in the Waterthorn tribe. He led the raid on the camp himself, while the other half of his army engaged the warriors. Out of the corner of his eye, Turnatt noticed some birds flying to the top of the highest tree. One held a small, shining object in his beak. Turnatt paid no mind. His soldiers had rounded up a dozen birds, mostly young birds and nesting females, and were busy putting their legs in cuffs and fighting back the few that tried to resist.

Much to Turnatt's surprise, some birds began singing a song. The rest, though outnumbered, still bravely struggled with Turnatt's soldiers. Again the shining thing caught the hawk's eye. This time it was even brighter, sending rays of light right through the clouds. What foolish trick was this?

Suddenly a flash as bright as lightning streaked across the forest. Turnatt looked around. There were no rain clouds. Instead in the sky hovered a huge bird. He was pure white, like snow, like clouds, like the foam of the waves of the sea. He had a long sword in his claws. To Turnatt's shock,

the bird was much larger than he was.

"Release the robins of the Waterthorn," the bird said in a booming voice.

What? Give up his hard-earned slaves just because the bird said so? Nobird could tell Turnatt what he should do.

Turnatt glared at the bird. "Who do you think you are, talking to me like that?" he bellowed.

The white bird made no movement. "Release the robins," he repeated in the same calm voice.

Turnatt didn't like it at all. He was a lord, a tyrant! The bird should bow down before him, not command him! "No! Go away!" Turnatt laughed and, with one swipe of his claw, knocked aside a robin who flung herself at him.

"No?" the white bird questioned, stretching the syllable.

Turnatt didn't answer. The next thing he knew, the bird had unfolded his large white wings to their full extent, raised his sword, and pointed it at him. Again there was a streak of light. Turnatt screeched in pain. He felt for a moment that his left eye was on fire, a fire that would never die. Turnatt knew he had greatly underestimated the white bird. He could barely see to fight. What if the bird blinded his remaining eye? Turning back, he fled with his crows and ravens.

All of the slavebirds he'd caught were lost, except one that was smuggled away, a thin robin with shining eyes and long, skinny legs. He was called Miltin. Yet he had been expensive. The lives of eighty-four of Turnatt's soldiers, not to mention the hawk lord's left eye, were gone in exchange for one little slavebird.

The hawk lord woke up with a start; the old dream had haunted him again. Infuriated, he smashed the empty eggshell in front of him. *Slavebirds!* They were the cause of all his troubles. As soon as Slime-beak came back, Turnatt would send him to check on the slavebirds' compound and make sure they were not up to anything. After all, you couldn't be too careful.

Victory is sweet, but one must remember
the sacrifices that bought it.
—FROM THE *OLD SCRIPTURE*

12
Remains of Victory

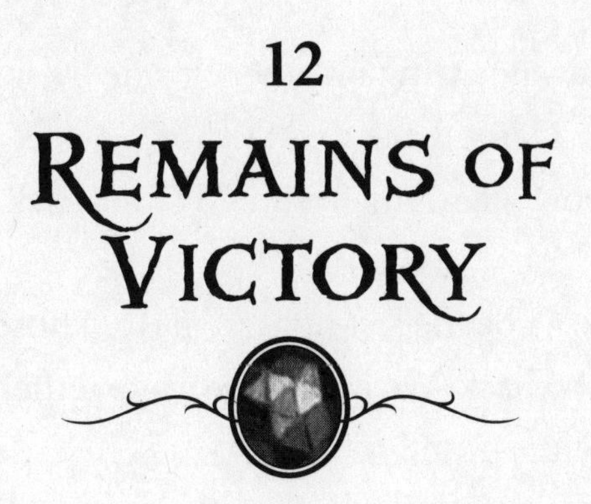

At the Appleby Hills it was pitch black, but all the red and the blue could see was brightness. They had won the fight with only a little loss.

"Well," grumbled Parrale, assessing the damage in the green and white hot-air balloon, "even a tiny hole in our balloon might delay us for days, let alone these holes. This won't fly for at least a week."

Near the food table Lorpil sniffled and blew his beak in a handkerchief. "Oh, all the beautiful, tasty food, gone!"

Farther away, sitting on a bench side by side, were the two leaders, Flame-back and Skylion.

"You know what, my friend?" Flame-back said.

"What?"

"This won't be the last fight we have. Those crows and ravens will be back. We need to work together if we want to defend Stone-Run."

The blue jay leader patted the cardinal's shoulder gently. "We do," he said simply. "And we will."

Across the battlefield a few blood-covered bodies of the crows and ravens littered the ground. Among them, some brave fighters of the red and the blue had gone to Sky Land and left their bodies behind. Of course, there was also bean soup spattered over the grass, pie fillings of all kinds glued onto trees and chairs, along with nuts here and there in the most unexpected places.

A few groups of cardinals and blue jays were out in the field, carrying stretchers. Lanterns were always nearby, like stars guiding the rescue groups back through the darkness.

Except for small fragments of quiet conversations, the whole place—the tallest mound on the Appleby Hills—

was filled with the chirping of the crickets hidden all over the battlefield. There wasn't any fancy music to celebrate the victory. Only the crickets sang, but that was enough.

Glenagh entered his study, stifling a yawn as he closed the branch door. What had happened that night was on his mind: not the attack but something else.

The birds in the play called Swordbird, and he came, the old blue jay mused. *Those crows and ravens will be back; my bones tell me so. And next time we may not be so lucky. How can we find the right way to call Swordbird, too?*

He reached up for a book on one of his shelves: the *Old Scripture*, Volume 2. The pages crackled as he turned to the beginning, Ewingerale's diary.

> LATE WINTER, "THE DAY OF SNOWFLAKES"
>
> *On the day when snowflakes started to swirl all around, we began our quest.*
>
> *I am Ewingerale the woodpecker, the son of Antoine Verne and Primrose. Since most birds call me Winger, it is not odd that I stick to the nickname and think of it as my only name. It fits me well because of my love for flight. Everybird I meet says that I am an*

undersized and bony woodpecker but have unusually large wings. I guess they are right. I always felt that my large wings were born to have a big use, so when I heard of Wind-voice's great quest, I joined it without hesitation.

EARLY SPRING, "THE DAY OF WINTER JASMINES"

Wind-voice says that on every quest, there is a bud, a flower, and a fruit. Our quest so far has gone well, so Wind-voice says that the flower has bloomed, a wonderful flower.

Our quest is to try to find and enliven all seven Leasorn gems across the world and to find a sword with the eighth Leasorn on its hilt. Wind-voice, the leader of our little group, seeks the sword because his mother told him to do so. Although Wind-voice has never seen the bird who sired him, his mother told him that his father was always watching over him. So we started off, three in all, to find the sword.

EARLY SPRING, "THE DAY OF HEROES"

What makes a hero? Bravery, strength, ability, and a heart for justice.

Wind-voice says that he wants to protect innocent birds from evil, to be a hero. In fact he isn't boasting;

he indeed looks like a hero: powerful and lean, with sparkling eyes. He looks like a dove, yet he's stronger and mightier than any dove who has ever flown. He has the skills to be a hero too. He is not only good at swordplay but also smart, quick to learn new things, and thoughtful of others. Crows cringe when they see him; even the intensity of the rain seems to lessen in his presence. And that's the very thing that has made me realize: If Wind-voice is able to find the Leasorn sword, there will be more happiness, more peace in all the forests.

Being tired, I cannot write more. Wind-voice, our hero, may you succeed!

Glenagh was reluctant to close the book. His interest was deeply aroused because the diary's author was Ewingerale, the companion of Wind-voice. Seasons later Wind-voice became a true hero—Swordbird.

Swordbird . . . the word rang in the head of the old blue jay. Something in his mind stirred, and Glenagh remembered what Skylion had told him: *Swordbird could solve this conflict.*

The old blue jay thought about it as he buried his head in the feathers of his left wing. Somewhere in the *Old Scripture* there must be the song to summon Swordbird. He would find it. Then, if they could ever find a Leasorn gem, they could call for help. And Swordbird would surely come.

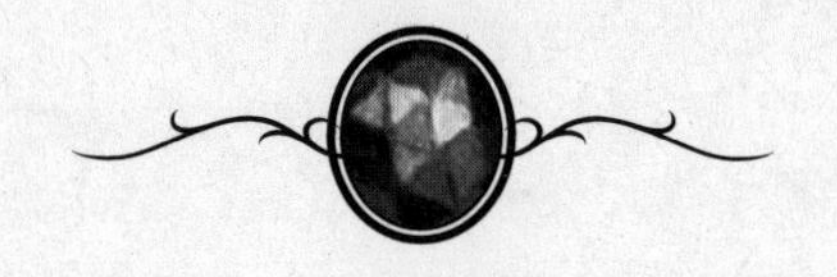

Remove the chains on our wings; we want to fly.
No matter how dim the hope is, we want to try.
Soon no longer slavebirds we shall be.
We shall be birds of joy, forever free.
Now we must trudge in the darkness of fear,
With only stars as companions,
But then freedom is near.
Left claw, right claw, farther into the night,
Soon the light of dawn came into sight.
Free at last, free at last . . .
Rejoice, the days of sorrow have passed.

—FROM A SONG IN THE *OLD SCRIPTURE*

13
ESCAPE

Midnight came quickly. The first-shift compound guard had gone back to his bed; the second-shift guard was now dead with darts in his throat. "Good shot!" Miltin congratulated Glipper. The slavebirds stepped over the body and left the compound. Tilosses used the knife to work their legs free.

Glipper came to the front of the line of birds to lead them. As he looked at the sky, he noticed that it had become cloudy. *Yes, that's good. The moon is bright enough for us to travel, yet not so bright that guards can take notice.* He looked back and saw Miltin give him a wing tip–up. That meant the robin had placed the bird dummies, and all was well at the back of the slavebird group. He returned the signal and started to crawl faster. The slavebirds uttered no sound in spite of the painful jagged rocks.

Glipper soon reached the hut. He and Miltin first helped the old and weak birds fly up to the hut roof. After everybird was safe, they made sure that no signs were left on the ground. The flycatcher and the robin were the last to fly up.

"It's time," Glipper said in a hushed tone to Tilosses. He, along with Miltin and the vireo brothers, crept to the edge of the roof and jumped noiselessly to the ground. They tipclawed nearer,

nearer to the gate. There were two guards. One of them was half dozing; the other had covered his eyes with his cap.

Miltin gestured left and right with his claw. "Glipper, attack Crooked-shoulder with me. You two can get Large-cap. Remember, silent as shadows, and stifle them with the rags!"

The other three nodded and vanished to their places, waiting for the right moment.

Miltin burst out of the darkness and threw his weight on Crooked-shoulder. The crow had the wind whacked out of him, so he uttered no more than a gasp. Glipper came close behind and stuffed a smelly old rag down his throat just as Miltin gave him a kick that knocked him cold.

Meanwhile, one of the vireo brothers slipped up and punched Large-cap in the face, followed by a blow to the stomach by the other brother. The guard collapsed to the ground without a sound.

The four signaled the rest of the slavebirds to follow. The others slid down the roof as quietly as possible and flew over the gate in twos and threes.

Soon the slavebirds were outside Fortress Glooming.

The slavebirds went north, remaining in the shadows. Nobird looked back to the nightmarish Fortress

Glooming, not even once.

Blood pounded in Miltin's ears. *Freedom is near,* he thought with a burst of excitement.

The faint moonlight shone on the slavebirds, kindly guiding them. Shadows were friends, greeting them, hiding them.

After a while a few birds gathered their courage to speak.

"How far is it now?" Glipper asked Miltin.

"Not very far, I suppose," came the hushed reply. The dreamy smell of rich earth mixed with pine needles greeted the birds' nostrils as the midnight breeze softly blew.

Crickets sang softly somewhere far off. "Free, free, free . . ." they seemed to chirp. The heartbeats of the slavebirds thumped along to the rhythm of the cricket calls.

Free, free, free . . .

"Stop!" Miltin suddenly hissed to the rest of the slavebirds behind him. They stumbled to a halt. "Somebird's coming this way!"

The slavebirds all froze in fright. Only their eyes moved. Yes, in the distance there were sounds of wings against the wind and claws crunching on leaves. They came closer.

"Don't move. It must be Slime-beak and his soldiers!" Glipper whispered. The slavebirds crouched stock-still, all hoping that the bushes and shadows were thick enough to hide them. No one dared to draw a breath, and all feared that the crows and ravens could hear the wild thumping of their hearts.

Nearer the crows and ravens came. Flickers of light indicated the torches that some soldiers held. The slavebirds could almost see the malicious eyes of the foul bunch glittering in the darkness. The first few crows and ravens brushed by, followed by another, and another. More flew overhead. Almost every one of them had a sharp spear. The smell of beans came from them, mixed with the stench of blood and burned feathers. Though there were about thirty crows and ravens, to the slavebirds it seemed as if the line were endless. It seemed like an eternity before the last of the regiment—a bony, mean-looking raven with a knife in his claw—passed by.

Miltin sighed in relief. The danger was over.

Tilosses coughed and quickly pressed his beak against his chest feathers to muffle the sound. But it was too late. The scrawny raven spun around, throwing his knife at the noise. The long blade whirled as it sliced through the air, moonlight gleaming on it. It struck the bark of the tree that Tilosses was leaning on, barely an inch from the old bird's throat. Not a single slavebird moved.

Narrowing his eyes as he scanned the darkness, the raven quietly walked toward Tilosses. His clawsteps were the only sounds in the night.

He stopped right before the bush that concealed Glipper. Glipper crouched lower and pressed his head to the ground. The other slavebirds were horror-stricken. Yet they could do nothing. The raven looked right and left.

Miltin was hiding in the shadow of an elm tree only a few clawsteps away. He picked up a round stone without making any sound and stood up very carefully. Everything was silent and still. All of a sudden he threw the stone as far as he could and then ducked down.

The thump of the stone on crisp leaves drew the raven's attention. He turned sharply and rushed toward the stone, which was a safe distance from the slavebirds. He found nothing, of course.

The raven growled to himself, taking a last look at the trees and shadows where the slavebirds were hiding. Then he jogged off to catch up with the rest of Slime-beak's regiment. His figure soon became a tiny speck in the distance.

Slime-beak and his battered troops finally arrived at the gate of Fortress Glooming. It wasn't a pretty sight, half the soldiers hopping, walking, or running and the other half flying. The captain knew he would be in deep trouble. When he had set out to battle, he'd had about fifty soldiers in all. When he retreated, there was only a sad number of thirty or so.

Normally Slime-beak would fly over the tall gate, but because his wings were sticky with bean soup, he had to call the guards at the other side of the gate. "You, in there! Open up!" Slime-beak called. No response. "Guards! No sleeping. You hear?"

Sensing that something was wrong, the captain sent a raven to check on the guards. Moments later, the raven croaked, "The guards are tied up and unconscious."

"They—slavebirds!" The words caught in the captain's throat. He dashed away to check the slave compound.

Slime-beak rushed into the musty, reeking place and tripped over something soft near the entrance. It was the body of the compound guard. Horrified, he stood up and looked around. There seemed to be lumps and bird-shaped shadows, but something was not quite right. It was quiet. Too quiet.

"Come on, sleepyheads! Get up and follow me!" There were no replies, only echoes. Slime-beak tore the sheet from a slavebird's bed, uncovering a reed-made dummy. He howled with rage. Bug-eye, the slave driver, was nowhere around.

"Soldiers!" Slime-beak ordered. "Use your skills now, and find those slavebirds! If you don't catch them, I'll use your hides to make shoes! Come on! Look! You miserable bunch of featherballs!"

The soldiers rushed out in different directions, investigating shadows and listening for noises.

Slime-beak quickly scrubbed and dried his wings. Then he led a squad and flew some distance before landing and investigating. One of his crows squinted at some moving shapes not far off. "What are those?" another soldier asked, holding a lantern in his claw.

Seeing the shapes moving rapidly away, Slime-beak charged at them. "Quick! Get the escaping slavebirds!"

When Glipper heard the crashes and the yells of the pursuing soldiers, he made a quick decision.

"I'll be the rear guard," Glipper said to Miltin. "You lead. No ifs and buts. Go! Hiding means nothing now!"

The slavebirds flew as fast as they could. Arrows whistled by their ears. A few unfortunate birds were hit and fell to the ground.

Slime-beak called out to his birds: "Soldiers! Fly to the other end and surround the slaves! Make sure no one escapes or I'll peel your hides and send you all to Sky Land!"

The soldiers quickly obeyed, filling up the sky. In a flash, screams pierced the air as the slavebirds were caught.

Miltin felt a stab of pain in his shoulder and he crashed to the ground. He grimaced. An arrow shaft was sticking out. Through the shock of being wounded, the robin glimpsed a clump of dense, tall bushes by the dim light of the moon. He looked right and left. Nobird was paying attention to him. Silent as a shadow, he vanished behind the bushes and crouched there, waiting. He held a bloody claw over the wound, panting slightly. Behind him Miltin could hear the haunting screams and yells of other slavebirds. He closed his eyes momentarily, taking in big breaths. Though Miltin yearned to fight side by side with the other slavebirds, his instincts told him to stay put, for he knew he could only save them by finding Aska's tribe. Gradually the screams and noises faded and died away; only then did Miltin open his eyes.

The night was noiseless now; the crickets sang no more. Only Miltin's labored breathing broke the silence. He felt his bloody wound. *I cannot stay here; it's unsafe!* Miltin clenched his claw around the arrow and pulled it out. He took a deep breath and tried to fly once more. But his wounded shoulder failed him and he dropped again. The pain worsened. He forced himself to get up and started to stagger north. Blood flowed down his side in thick streams, so he grabbed a dock leaf in his beak and pressed it to his shoulder.

He did not know how long he had been stumbling, and the pain grew worse with every step. Blood throbbed in his head, almost pounding his brain to bits. Thoughts whirled inside. *Glipper and Tilosses . . . Aska and her tribe . . . Fortress Glooming . . . peace . . . freedom . . .*

Suddenly Miltin tripped over a stone and fell face-down. He didn't bother to get up, just lay in the dirt with his eyes closed. Oh, he was tired. Oh, his wounded shoulder hurt. Though his feet still kicked wildly as if running, his efforts were in vain. Blood had covered his right shoulder and a part of his right wing and had now dried in layers. Despite his tiredness, he struggled to rise once more. The pain was too intense; tears squeezed out of his eyes as he tried. Panting, he lifted his head a little. In the distance he could make out a camp of some sort. He was tired. So tired. Darkness began to take over Miltin's mind. "Freedom!"—that was the last word he wanted to shout out, just before he fell unconscious.

Off we go to the mountaintop,
What lies ahead we do not fear.
No obstacle will make us stop,
Till we reach the land so dear.
May the wind under our wings
Be smooth and fair on this journey!

—FROM EWINGERALE'S DIARY IN THE *OLD SCRIPTURE*

14
The Leasorn Gem

Miltin opened his eyes with a feeble moan. He heard a voice: "Miltin!"

He smiled weakly as he recognized a face. "Aska," he managed to whisper. His questioning look prodded her to explain.

She gestured to a far-off place through the branches. "My tribe found you not far from the northwest shore of the Silver Creek, unconscious. We managed to get you here and call for a medicine bird. I expect him to arrive any minute now. *Hmm* . . . since you've escaped, no doubt there will be trouble from that hawk again."

Miltin let the information sink into his brain. He immediately sat up, in spite of his wounded shoulder. "I must go at once!" he declared.

The medicine bird and Glenagh came in just at that moment. They looked strangely at the robin.

"Where do you need to go?" questioned Aska, thinking that Miltin had become slightly delirious.

Miltin blinked several times, rubbed his eyes, and sighed. "To my home, the Waterthorn, of course. I must! The red gem . . ."

"What gem? Why?"

Miltin slouched, but his eyes shone brighter than ever. They seemed to see nothing yet everything. "I must . . . my friends—the slavebirds—they need it . . . so does your tribe. . . . I must! The red Leasorn! Let me take you to get the gem and call for Swordbird!" Miltin paused and panted with the effort of speaking. His voice faded to a whisper. "Call for him! Let Swordbird come!" With that, the robin collapsed back into his bed, exhausted.

Aska was silent for a moment and then turned to the elder, Glenagh, in confusion.

The old blue jay went into a spiritlike trance. His eyes grew bright as he murmured: "The Leasorn gem! The valuable gem of the Great Spirit!" He gazed up at the sky for a moment, his face illuminated with joy.

The medicine bird who had been examining Miltin's wounds was surprised by the actions of the elder. "You scared me for a second, old Glen." He took out a bandage from his bag. "What's all this about the Leasorn gem and Swordbird?" Aska looked puzzled too.

"Oh, dear friend, don't you see? To make Swordbird come we need to learn the song, and we also need a Leasorn gem. However, legends say that there are only seven gems on the earth and another on Swordbird's sword!"

Aska gasped. "You mean, Miltin's family, the Waterthorn tribe, has a Leasorn!"

The medicine bird paused as he looked up. He met Glenagh's excited gaze. "The problem of Turnatt is solved!"

Glenagh smiled widely. "Not yet, my friend, but soon!" He put a wing tip to the robin's shoulder. "Thank you, Miltin!" he whispered as he left the room. "How the birds at the meeting will rejoice at this information!"

The meeting was held not far from Miltin's room, at a branch that curved into a perfect oval. Many important birds perched on it. Smaller twigs stretched off into the oval, covering the hole in the middle and making a suitable table after a tablecloth was draped on top.

The red and the blue were arguing and discussing when Glenagh made his appearance. "I have the solution, ladies and gentlebirds!" he declared, wings spreading out. The noisy talking ceased immediately. All eyes turned to Glenagh. "Our only chance to fight off the hawk and survive is to call for Swordbird."

Flame-back, the cardinal leader, spoke with urgency. "Quite right. We have no other choice since most of us believe that Turnatt will launch a second attack. We must try to prevent him from doing further damage to our

Stone-Run. In order to do so, we need to learn the song and find the Leasorn gem."

"I'm translating the song," Glenagh said.

"But the Leasorn!" The cardinal leader went on. "How in the name of Swordbird are we going to find such a rare gem?"

Glenagh's smile became very wide. "Ah, that was what I was coming to. Our friend, Miltin, the robin, knows how."

"How?" the meeting members asked in unison.

"His family, the Waterthorn tribe, who live beyond the White Cap Mountains, has a Leasorn."

The red and the blue turned silent. Outside, leaves rustled as the wind grew stronger.

"We must pick a few who will fly on a mission to borrow the Leasorn," Skylion proclaimed solemnly. "It won't be easy. The mountains are high and desolate, and those robbers the Sklarkills haunt the passes. We must choose birds who can withstand all dangers to protect the Leasorn, birds who can be of good health even without food and water for days."

"Aye, that's for sure," murmurs came from the meeting members.

"I'll go." Cody spoke earnestly. "I would like to do anything I can for Stone-Run."

"And I'll go with him," Brontë added. "Two are better than one."

"They are both kindhearted lads," the birds whispered among themselves.

"Aye, they are."

Just then a voice pierced the air. "No, I will!" Aska cried. Her eyes shone with determination and bravery. She stepped through the doorway and looked at the silent crowd.

Glenagh turned around in surprise. "And why is that, young lady?" He shook his head slowly as he looked up and down at the blue jay. "Can you survive the dangers of the White Cap Mountains? Can you withstand hunger and thirst if supplies run out? Can you make your way through all the obstacles?"

Aska bowed her head. "I can," she whispered.

It was only a second before she suddenly stood tall, and her eyes opened, filled with love for Stone-Run. Her voice became louder and stronger with every word. "I can! Being a girl doesn't mean I can't stand these hardships. I should be the one to go. Why, here, two strong, able-bodied warriors are willing, but they shouldn't go. They are needed here. Who will defend the old, the young, the sick, and the disabled when they are gone? Who will stop Turnatt if he plans a second attack and tries to destroy Stone-Run once and for all? They are our protectors. They should not leave for such a task. I can get the Leasorn. Besides, Miltin will go with me; he knows the way." She breathed hard as she finished her speech and shifted her gaze from one bird to another.

The meeting members were silent for a second. Then a small wave of clapping gradually turned into a thunderous applause. Tears were in some birds' eyes, they were so moved by the speech.

"Well said, lass. Well said," declared Skylion. Cody and Brontë agreed.

"Let's go tomorrow!" A new voice pierced the air. Miltin had staggered into the room, shocking everyone into silence.

Aska sent a questioning look to Skylion.

There was a pause. "Yes, you can, Aska and Miltin. I give you that permission with pleasure," Skylion said. "But not tomorrow. Miltin needs at least a day or two to recover his strength."

Aska felt her heart soar in the sky. *I can do it!* she thought.

I've never seen any mountains quite like the White Cap Mountains. They are called so because the tops of them are covered by mists, mists so thick that from a distance you cannot see the tops. Though coniferous forests cover the visible part of the mountains, the tops are barren. What dwell in the mountains I cannot say. "Monsters," was the reply of a bird living near them when I asked him.

—FROM EWINGERALE'S DIARY IN THE *OLD SCRIPTURE*

15
SURMOUNTING THE WHITE CAP MOUNTAINS

The top of the White Cap Mountains was a ghastly place. Trees were scattered across the misty landscape like ghosts. Aska and Miltin had been confident when they started to fly up the slopes in the morning, but now they were not so sure.

"Oh, you can hardly see anything from here." Aska squinted at a shadow in the distance. "What is that? A tree, or a boulder maybe? Or something . . . else?"

Miltin shrugged. "Who knows? Let's avoid it." So the two birds veered around the shadow. They had never before seen such a thick fog; everything around them seemed to be covered by a milk-white veil.

The two soared in absolute silence. Miltin flew with steady, measured stokes, refusing to favor his aching wing, but his heart was beating furiously. Aska dared not talk; she focused on flying as fast and as deliberately as she could. A stretch of time followed, and though it was only minutes, it seemed to be hours until Miltin spoke.

"I-I think our minds played a trick on us. I don't see anything anywhere." His words were half true. Of course they hadn't seen anything suspicious, but how could they see anything clearly in the fog?

Aska smiled nervously. "I hope you're right, Miltin. I don't like this place at all. Remember what Skylion told us? The Sklarkills could be sneaking right behind—"

"Stop! Stop! Let's not make the situation harder than it already is."

They fell silent again. Every so often a frightening shadow would appear in the distance, only to be revealed as a twisted dead tree or an uneven lump of rock deposited there by avalanches long ago.

No wind blew on the very top of the mountains, and no trees rustled their leaves. In truth there were no leaves to rustle, for the only trees were stiff conifers and dead ones as dry and old as the mountains themselves. No grass grew, only thick carpets of moss covering the rocky ground. The moist air caressed the land with its icy fingers, leaving drops of water behind. There were waterlogged depressions in the earth, some as small as a plate and some as large as a basin, which were like countless still mirrors reflecting the fog. No ripple ever came to their surface; nobird disturbed them.

Minutes went by, and Aska and Miltin soared over a ravine, a sight that was both horrifying and breathtaking. Though the mist did not allow them to see the entire chasm, the edges and the feeling of emptiness were enough.

Aska suddenly tensed. Miltin glanced quickly around. "What is it?"

"There's . . . well, a rhythmic sound, coming closer. . . ."

"What? I didn't hear a thing. Maybe it's just your imagination—"

Aska quickly cut the robin off. "No, stop beating your wings like a madbird. Fly slowly. Now can you hear it?" Aska's face was strained with fear.

Miltin's eyes grew bigger. "Yes, quite clearly. Why, they're saying . . ."

There was chanting in the distance. It got louder and

louder and soon surrounded the two travelers, echoing in the mist.

"Sklarkills! Sklarkills! Kill, kill, kill! Give us your treasures or you'll die!"

Miltin beat his wings faster than ever. But there was no way out; the strange birds had encircled them thoroughly, unnoticed because of the fog. The bandits closed in on them.

"We don't have any treasures," Aska shouted.

"Sklarkills! Sklarkills! Kill, kill, kill! Give us whatever you have!" they yelled darkly. Now Aska could see that the Sklarkills were large jackdaws who had shimmering snakeskin vests with swirling green patterns on them. Some even wore headbands to match.

Miltin took a silent count. His eyes widened with worry. "Dozens of them at least. We're hopelessly outnumbered, Aska! Our only way out is up."

"But the air is thin up there! We could suffocate!"

"It's all we can do." Miltin's face was grim. "Here. A saber to protect yourself with. I'll be okay with a rapier. Don't worry if we get separated. Just go!"

The two birds armed themselves and darted up through layers of fog. Sklarkill jackdaws followed, bellowing in anger, trying to block their way. They thrust long spears at the two travelers. One of the spears tore

Miltin's carrying pack. Supplies spilled out, and Miltin was thrown off-balance. Down he spun, into the mob of the eager jackdaws. The Sklarkills stabbed and pierced him with their spears, threatening to close in. Miltin whirled his rapier furiously, blocking as many spears as possible. Yet he couldn't hold out for long. Aska knocked a Sklarkill jackdaw back with her saber and came thundering down. She slashed with all her might, roaring into her enemies' faces, using her small size to duck the wild stabs of the spears. Then Miltin regained his balance, and they struggled to fly upward.

"Hold your breath and fly higher!" Miltin urged, wind whistling in his feathers. "Higher!" They flew up and up. The Sklarkills followed, still chanting their threatening song, "Kill, kill! Sklarkills, kill!" No matter how high they went, the Sklarkills always followed. When Aska gasped for breath, her lungs felt as though they were on fire.

"Down. Now!" Miltin whispered dryly. The two plunged down, waving their weapons as they dived. Aska was not seriously wounded; she had only a small slash on her back and tiny nicks and sores. Miltin, on the other wing, was bleeding all over. With the speed of their dive, the two managed to evade the mob. Yet it was only a temporary escape. The Sklarkills quickly followed them.

"Aska," Miltin gasped, "follow me! Quick!"

"What? Why are we—"

"Don't ask now. You'll see later. Just follow!" The robin flew with a burst of speed back the way they had come. Aska zoomed closely behind, a little confused. Why were they heading back when they were almost on the other side of the mountains? The Sklarkill band was in hot pursuit.

Miltin glanced back. "Take this, jackdaws!" he hollered, and snatched a large bag of grain out of his torn pack. He threw it as far as he could.

Immediately, the jackdaws flew to the bag, fighting for it, yelling to one another in hoarse voices, "Mine! Mine!"

Miltin kept flying. Suddenly the ravine again opened up beneath the robin and the blue jay. Rapidly Miltin and Aska turned and plunged into it. They disappeared in the mist. "Keep to the cliffs and sides!" Miltin whispered. "Quick! The Sklarkills will catch up soon!"

Miltin's eyes darted to and fro. He kept glancing at the jagged cliffs that were the borders of the ravine.

"Here!" Miltin whispered urgently. He flew headlong into a small cranny in the cliff. It was just big enough for him and Aska. Inside it was dry and dusty. Dark too.

Now the fog worked to Aska and Miltin's advantage. The Sklarkills could not see where their victims had gone. The blue jay and the robin huddled together, listening intently, until the last of the threatening chants faded in the distance.

Miltin breathed a sigh of relief. "That's over," he said.

"Watch out!" Aska cried.

A skinny young Sklarkill, more persistent than the rest of his band, had been hunting along the ravine for any place the two fugitives might have hidden. Now he poked his head and one foot into the cranny, snapping at Miltin's tail. "Give me what you have!" he screeched.

Miltin spun around, rapier in claw. The jackdaw let out a horrible shriek as the blade crashed down between his eyes. He slumped and started to slip backward out of the hole, the weight of his paralyzed body pulling him down.

But as he fell, his claw hooked on to Miltin's tunic. The jackdaw plummeted down through the swirling, misty air, dragging Miltin with him.

"Aska!" The cry of the robin hung in the air. It was followed by a sickening thud.

Miltin awoke, pain grasping every part of his body. Even opening his eyes was painful. He slowly craned his neck and looked around. He was in a cave! To his right was the cave entrance; to his left were a small fire and Aska.

He groaned as the soreness stung again. "What happened, Aska? Where am I? I hardly remember anything except that I fell. . . ."

Aska nodded. "Yes, you fell, yelling my name. My heart was in my throat! I couldn't possibly bear to fly down to see you smashed by the force of that fall."

Miltin smiled weakly. "Well, you did."

"I did. You were not smashed at all! How happy I was to find you alive, in one piece! You landed on that Sklarkill. I moved you to this cave, which is at the bottom of the ravine. Then it rained. Look, it's only a small drizzle now."

"But . . . I'll bet that our rations are gone too."

Aska sadly nodded.

Silently, the two listened to the light, whispering rain.

"It's time for the colors of evilness,"
he harshly whispered, eyes glinting with fire.
"Red, of blood and flame;
Black, of shadow and night."

—FROM A STORY IN THE *BOOK OF HERESY*

16
A Ball of Fire

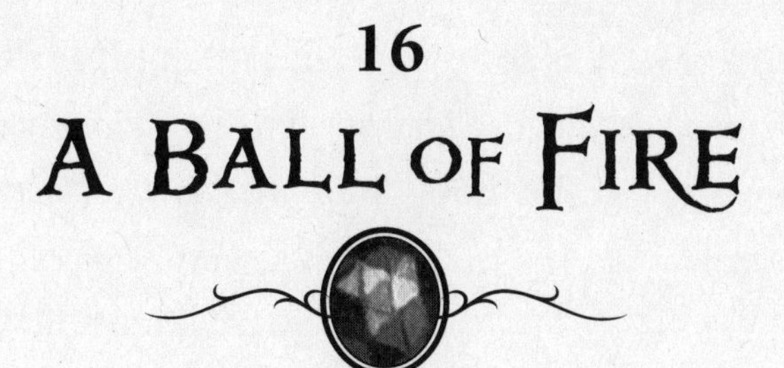

Turnatt's temper had gone from bad to worse. How could he not be angry when he saw Slime-beak returning battered and beaten? The captain looked as if he had swum in soup and jumped on pies.

He begged for mercy as some pie filling dripped down his face. "Oh, Milord, there were a couple of trick-sters among the woodbirds! Some horrible birds who attacked us with food! Though I was defeated by the woodbirds, I caught the escaping slaves as I came back. Oh, forgive me, milord!" Slime-beak knelt down low at Turnatt's claws.

Turnatt eyed his soup-covered captain. *If I kill him or demote him, I can't find another bird in my army capable of taking his place,* he thought. *Besides, I might need to use him later.*

Still, Turnatt was disgusted with the crow's appearance and roared to his soldiers to take the whimpering Slime-beak away. He did not want the food-covered captain to make a mess on his fine polished marble floor.

The stupidity of Bug-eye, nursing his injured claw in the infirmary while the slaves escaped, along with the defeat of Slimebeak at the Appleby Hills, infuriated the hawk lord. His angry thoughts whirled and churned like a hurricane. Turnatt was not the kind of bird who kept his anger to himself. His yellow eye became brighter and brighter, as though it were a ball of fire. Soon it grew so frightening that the soldiers on guard in his chamber looked away, shivering. All of the hawk lord's feathers rose, making him twice his original size. His deadly talons flexed; his cruel beak sliced through the air.

Just then an innocent soldier sneezed, and suddenly Turnatt could not bear it any longer. Faster than lightning, his claws stuck out and his beak dug into the bird's flesh. The raven died instantly, but Turnatt kept ripping the body apart. His movements were so swift that the cringing soldiers could not see him clearly. But they could well hear the growls and bellows and the sound of flesh and bone being torn apart. They stood as far away as they could, frightened to silence.

Turnatt brutally feasted on the raven's flesh and drank his blood. He grinned at his soldiers as if they were friends.

"Give each slavebird twenty lashes." He tapped his covered eye slowly. His other eye narrowed into a slanted slit. "Get me Shadow now, and then you're dismissed."

The soldiers went away. Turnatt heard the screams of the slavebirds being beaten outside when the raven scout slipped in. "Yes, Your Majesty?" Shadow played with the edge of his black cloak. His amber eyes glowed as he peered at the hawk.

"Since I trust you, you'll be put on the biggest job of your life. If you fail, you'll die!" Turnatt began the conversation with a threat. "Now, how many good scouts are available?"

"Ten counting myself, Your Majesty," Shadow answered, closing one eye.

"Good. You'll lead an attack on those cardinals and blue jays. Get your scouts ready, and get a bottle of oil or two. Prepare to set fire to those filthy woodbirds' camps! Do as much damage as you can. I'll also give you some archerbirds to command. Do not be foolish, and don't let me see you covered in beans like that scum Slimebeak when you come back!"

"You have my word as a scout, Your Majesty. I will not fail you."

Turnatt quickly cut the raven short. "Good! Now start!"

Over the next few days Shadow and his scouts observed the red and the blue, watching for their weaknesses. They gathered enough oil and other necessary supplies. They were the strong right wing of Turnatt's army, and they seldom failed to accomplish their tasks.

The day after Aska and Miltin's departure, Glenagh found what he was looking for, the "Song of Swordbird" in the fifth volume of the *Old Scripture*. But it was in the old language, which none of the birds could speak anymore. Glenagh painstakingly set about translating it.

"Sing it, Cody." Glenagh handed the paper to him. "Do you think we got it right this time?"

Cody started to sing.

There's a place we know that holds peace.
There's a time we know that treasures peace.
There's a reason we know why we want peace.
There's a bird we know who can create peace.
Swordbird, Swordbird!
Oh, let us have peace,
Oh, let us have freedom once more.
Let the evil be driven away.
Let the forest be filled with sunshine.
Make the land a peaceful place once more.
May peace and freedom be with birds forever.

Cody paused to catch his breath. "Is that all? I like the tune."

Glenagh shook his head as he adjusted his spectacles. "Only the first verse. I haven't got the second verse yet, but I'll bet we can find it."

"In time for Aska and Miltin's return, of course," said Cody.

"Yes, and I hope no serious trouble will come from Turnatt before that."

Shadow was hiding close to Glenagh's study. He noted the happenings with satisfaction. "You are looking for Swordbird's help now? Well, I'll see about that when flames devour your home and singe your song sheets! Will you be happy and sing then?" He vanished with the other scouts.

Cody rubbed his eyes. Things were strange lately. He had heard whispers that slowly faded into the sounds of the creek. He knew these might be coming from his imagination, but he had just now seen two amber eyes staring out of the darkness. As he looked harder, they vanished. He didn't think that his senses had played a trick on him. He was sure that somebird was watching silently. Deep down Cody knew something terrible was about to happen.

That evening, Shadow gave his last instructions to his band of scouts and archers. "Listen, my friends. Together, we are strong, but apart, we shall be defeated. The red and the blue can be powerful together, as Slime-beak discovered. But tonight the blue shall be alone and at our mercy. Burn, scouts! Destroy! As for the archers, stay in the shadows and make no moves till I say so!" He turned to a few of his scouts. "You three, pour oil on the exposed roots of the trees, and then set them aflame! Let the evening come, for it is our friend!" All the silent birds nodded and went to their work. They were so well camouflaged that nobird saw them as they prepared to kill.

Everything was calm in the Bluewingle camp until flames erupted. Cries of alarm came from the birds as they fled their nest rooms and trees, but some didn't get out in time. Yells shook the night as arrows sprang from the surrounding undergrowth. Since it was dark, nobird knew where the archers were. The fire grew more intense, until the camp trees looked as if they were made of burning gold. Branches crackled with tremendous noise, burned off, and crashed down, trapping some fleeing birds underneath. Cries hung in the air as arrows pierced throats and hearts. The night air was thick with screams and smoke.

Cody dashed out from his flaming home. He flew as fast as he could toward the Sunrise camp, knowing that their friends were their only hope.

Soon a band of cardinals, joined by the theater group and Cody, rushed to the scene, armed and ready to defend the blue jays against anything. But it was too late. The scouts and archers were gone like a gust of wind.

Bodies lay piled together. Some were killed, but most were just wounded. The ones who were alive were crying silently next to those who had fallen. Scorched feathers floated in the air. The whole tribe became a sea of flames.

Play the same old tricks whenever possible.

—FROM THE *BOOK OF HERESY*

17
Second Raid

As the cardinals and the theater birds watched helplessly, flames swallowed up the Bluewingle camp. But then a flash of lightning lit all the faces of the birds, followed by a deafening roll of thunder. Rain started to pour down and extinguished the fire within minutes.

Flame-back, Cody, and a few strong cardinals went into the remains of the camps to look for survivors. They found Glenagh trapped in a corner of his study, lying on a pile of charred books and documents, with his wings open to cover them. A deep cut over one eye was bleeding freely.

"Glen! Are you all right?" the cardinal leader cried.

"Oh . . . the song to call Swordbird . . . the *Old Scripture* . . . they're burned!" croaked Glenagh in a raspy voice.

Cody helped the old blue jay up. "Don't worry, Glen. I can still remember the first verse of the song."

"Our camp has a copy of the *Old Scripture* too, Glenagh," said Flame-back. "You'll all have to come back with us. Bring the wounded. You'll be safe there."

Shadow and his scouts and archers glided over the gate of Fortress Glooming and landed breathlessly on the steps of the main building. He dismissed his birds with a flick of a wing and dashed up the stairway to Turnatt's private chamber.

"Come in, scout," grumbled Turnatt.

Shadow respectfully bowed his head. "Yes, Your Majesty. We've burned the blue jays' camp and killed many blue jays with arrows. But when we returned to fetch some oil to burn the cardinals, it began to rain."

"Not bad," growled the hawk lord. "Attack the cardinals

tomorrow night if the rain stops. Beware, the woodbirds may have set up defenses."

"Yes. Thank you, Your Majesty. Good night, Your Majesty!" Shadow saluted the hawk and backed out of the room.

When the woodbirds and the theater members arrived at the cardinals' camp, the first thing they did was to clear out a nearby cave. This cave was a big one, with a small pond inside. The cardinals had often come here to drink the water because it was the sweetest for miles around. The birds piled some straw bedding around the pool and carried the wounded in. A medicine bird was called to tend them. The theater birds also escorted the hatchlings and the old, weak, sick, and disabled birds into the cave so that they could be sheltered if an attack came.

Flame-back and Skylion led a group of birds to hang nets around the camp trees. Although it was still raining outside, lightning and thunder became less frequent.

In the cardinals' tribe there were several large nets made out of a kind of sturdy weed. They were used for capturing dangerous animals that came too near for the cardinals' liking. Each was cone-shaped, with a thick rope tied at the end. The rope would be hung on a high branch, with the other end inside a room. As a beast came near, a bird would release the rope, and the nets would crash down.

The rain stopped, and in the eastern sky the first rays of sunlight shone.

After setting out sentries around the camp, Flame-back and Skylion went inside to discuss the next step.

"The enemies attacked my tribe at night, so they're likely to do the same again," Skylion reasoned. "Judging from the flames last night, I think that they poured oil on the lower part of the trunks before they set them on fire. So we must stop the birds one way or another before they do it."

Flame-back nodded. "Right. We have some nets, but they may not be enough."

"We certainly can station some archers," the blue jay leader said slowly. "But it would be even better if there were some gigantic spiderwebs—"

"Why, Skylion, you remind me! Have you ever used sticky-grass to catch winged insects to eat?" Flame-back asked.

"Do you mean the leafy grass with resinlike sap in the stems? Oh, yes, of course I have used it," Skylion said with interest. "When you break the stem, the sticky, clear glue will flow out. If you smear a bit on one branch and move the stem, it will make a sticky string. Apply the glue on another branch, stretch it and stick it on another, and another. . . .When finished, it will resemble a spiderweb. There always will be some mosquitoes and flies stuck in the web the next morning. Pick them out and you'll have a wonderful breakfast."

"We have lots of sticky-grass growing behind our camp, Skylion. Let's pick some and make webs all over the tribe-trees' branches! It would be much safer with these sticky webs," Flame-back suggested.

"Good idea! Let's get some birds to help us do that now!" Skylion couldn't wait.

Just as predicted, Shadow and his scouts showed up that night. They perched near the main tree, observing it through the leaves.

Shadow turned to his scouts. "You two set fire to the main tree. Be careful: There are birds awake there. Pour oil onto the base of the tree too."

"Yes, sir!" The two scouts flew off with two large buckets in their claws.

Shadow waited for quite a while, but there weren't any flames. He ordered the rest of his band to pour oil and set fire to the camp trees and let the archers follow the scouts to protect them from behind. Again nothing happened. At last he could not wait any longer and flew to the main tree to see what had gone wrong.

When he got close, he heard the halting cries of crows from sticky webs in the trees, and nets. He cursed and drew out an arrow, taking careful aim at a cardinal sentry. But just before he let the bowstring go, somebird else's arrow flew out of the darkness, brushing the feathers on his head. His shot went wild as he turned to face a large cardinal who swooped down from a branch. He had a bow in his claw and a quiver on his back, with knives and darts in his belt.

"I am Flame-back, leader of the Sunrise tribe," the cardinal said in a threatening voice. "Leave now and I will let you go with your life."

"Never, fool! Death to you!" Shadow hissed, and

lunged at him, saber flashing. Flame-back nimbly skipped away and with a twang shot another arrow at the scout. Shadow ducked, the shaft whistling by his ear. "Fight with me if you dare!" he growled. But Flame-back turned and flew out of his sight.

Furious, the scout dived after him. He came to another camp tree but didn't see the cardinal. He listened intently. Suddenly he snatched out a knife and threw it. The long knife first split an arrow that came from that direction and then landed with a muffled thud somewhere out of Shadow's sight. There was a soft moan. Shadow, his eyes shining with malice, eagerly rushed toward the sound. His black cape billowed behind him like a ghost.

The wounded Flame-back didn't give up. He yanked the knife out of his side and with a grunt used it to block a deathblow aimed at him from Shadow's saber. He scrambled up, and the two birds clashed in a blur of blades. Crows are naturally larger than cardinals, so Flame-back's chance of winning the battle was slim. But his angry face and the unusual amount of weaponry on him made Shadow a little uncertain. And Flame-back was extremely quick-clawed and agile, so before long the scout was breathing hard.

Neither seemed to gain an advantage as they parried

and thrust around the camp trees. The air filled with the clangs of metal.

Shadow laughed and managed to quickly wrench Flame-back's knife out of his claws, but just as fast Flame-back pulled out a scimitar and lunged at Shadow. The sudden movement caught Shadow off guard. The scout immediately lost his smile as a good number of feathers were chopped off, leaving a patch of skin bare.

Shadow was infuriated. "You'll pay for that, scalawag!" He charged at the cardinal again. The scout's saber sliced a piece of flesh from Flame-back's claw, and the cardinal dropped his scimitar in pain. Seeing his chance, Shadow aimed blow after blow at Flame-back, and the cardinal could only duck and retreat.

"Hold on! I'm coming, Flame-back!" Skylion rushed to join the battle. He tossed a sword to the cardinal leader, and together they battled with the scout. Two were too many for Shadow; he turned and fled. Flame-back and Skylion tailed behind.

"Here, raven!" Flame-back roared angrily, and shot dart after dart at him. One struck Shadow's behind, and the scout yelped, almost falling to the ground. But the dart hadn't gone deep, and Shadow flew even faster.

Flame-back gathered all the strength he had to rush

after the scout. He seized the raven's cape and pulled with all his might. Skylion joined him, and together they tried to yank Shadow back to the camp. They almost succeeded, but then the crafty scout cut his cape off with his saber.

After he had freed himself, Shadow spun around and aimed his saber at Flame-back. The cardinal leader ducked, but he was a little slow. The blade bit deep into his shoulder. Thrown off-balance, the cardinal fell to the ground.

Roaring, Skylion gave the scout a solid wing clout, battering his head.

Flame-back regained his balance and yelled, "Archers, fire!"

From the treetops nearby, heads of cardinals and blue jays popped out in neat rows, bowstrings drawn back. Shadow dropped his saber and tried to flee. Too late.

Bows went singing. Arrows whistled from all directions, piercing the scout's skin. With a horrendous shriek Shadow rose into the air. He disappeared into the night, followed by another volley of arrows and angry shouts.

Skylion flew to Flame-beak. "I'm all right," the cardinal leader said. "My side is cut, and so is my shoulder. But they'll heal."

"I gave that raven a wing clout he won't soon forget,"

Skylion added. "Our archers did a wonderful job. He won't be around for a while."

Skylion and Flame-back were immediately surrounded by the Sunrise and Bluewingle warriors. When the red and the blue shifted their gaze to the crows and ravens trapped in the nets and webs, anger and hate boiled in their chests.

"Throw stones at them!" a blue jay roared. Many voices agreed.

"Don't, my friends," Skylion said gently. "They are now helpless and can't harm us. We will take them prisoner and release them one day, far from Stone-Run. But we cannot be murderers. They have a right to live, as do all creatures that fly, swim, or run on this beautiful earth. Swordbird would not wish us to wrench their lives away."

The place is full of sorrow;
There is no joy, no song.
There is a valley without a flower,
Feeling the wind go by.
There's a riverbed without water,
Forever and ever dry.
Everything seems so dreary; it feels just too airy,
But on the hill, there's a small wildflower that never cries.
Because hope is what it lives on.

—FROM A SONG IN THE *OLD SCRIPTURE*

18
Living on Hope

In the cave Aska bathed Miltin's wounds with spring-water, spread a mountain herb poultice on them, and bandaged them gently. Miltin smiled his thanks, and then his eyes drifted shut.

Realizing that Miltin urgently needed something to eat, Aska went outside to seek food. Crawling among the boggy puddles, the blue jay cropped the soft tips of new moss and put them in her bag. But then Asa spied a small golden blossom amidst the dull green, its petals fluttering in the light breeze. The blue jay stood there motionless, watching the flower bloom in the misty coldness. She knew every plant of the woodlands by heart, but she had never seen such a flower before.

"Oh, how could something so beautiful live here? Is it a magic plant sent by Swordbird?" Aska whispered. "Thank you, Swordbird! Miltin can be saved!" Aska dug out every bit of the flower with care and rushed back to the cave.

Aska put the golden flower and the moss into a pot of springwater over the fire and stirred them with a spoon. The pot boiled, giving off a delightful smell.

The roots, leaves, and petals bobbed in the soup as if they were saying temptingly, "Eat, eat. . . ."

Oh, how Aska wanted to taste it! "No! Miltin needs every drop of it to survive!" she told herself firmly.

She poured the soup into a bowl and gently woke the robin. Miltin attempted to hold the spoon, but he was too weak to do so. She fed him sip by sip. But after a spell Miltin refused to eat any more. "You need it to keep up your strength too!" he said.

"But you're injured! You need it more than I do."

"But who will gather food if you fall sick from starvation?" Miltin returned.

Aska laughed and agreed to sip a few spoonfuls yet left most of the soup for Miltin. Aska started to feed the robin again, and he meekly opened his beak to the soup spoon like a hatchling.

"It tastes . . . like spring . . ." Miltin whispered. He swallowed another beakful. "Like . . . like . . ."

"It's the taste of a golden flower, the taste of hope," the blue jay finished.

Miltin woke up early the next morning. To his surprise, the pain in his shoulder from the arrow wound had lessened, and the cuts and slashes from the Sklarkills' spears no longer burned and ached. He tried a practice flight and found that his wings worked nearly as well as before.

Miltin rushed back to the cave to tell Aska the good news. "Don't you think it's strange that I can fly again?" Miltin grinned. "Let's go out of the ravine and fly down the mountains now!"

I was right! Aska thought with wonder. *That golden flower must be a magical herb sent by Swordbird! Thank you again, Swordbird!*

Still, she was worried. Miltin seemed better and stronger, but his wounds were not completely healed. Aska forced him to wait until she finished checking and changing his bandages. The wound in his shoulder was the worst, deep and only half healed, and a long day of flying yesterday had already strained it.

The two set off.

The mist, as they went down the mountains, faded into a clear blue sky, so welcoming that it made Aska's heart sing and Miltin's heart soar.

"The Waterthorn tribe! Mother, Father, here I come!" Miltin yelled to the sunny forest below.

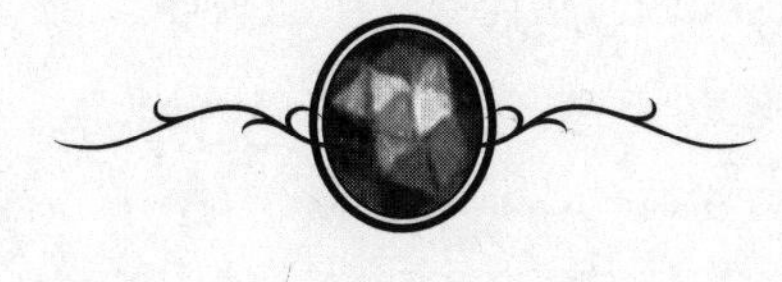

Those who died shall not have died in vain,
for they are brave souls fighting for rightness,
and he who guards peace and brings justice to the
world shall give them a rest they deserve.
—FROM THE *OLD SCRIPTURE*

19
MILTIN'S WISH

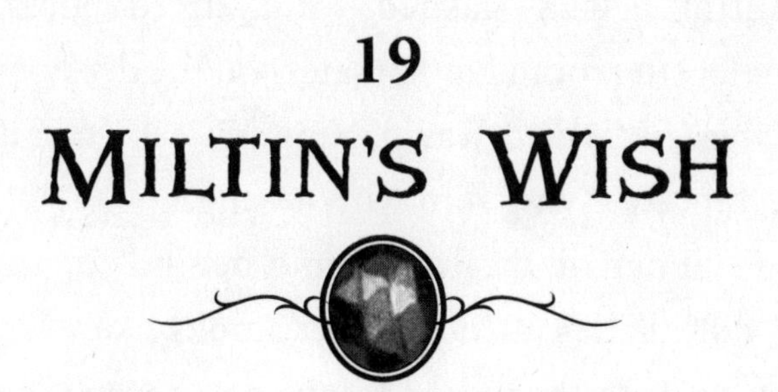

It was nearly noon when Aska and Miltin flew over a river.

"Look! That's the Rockwell River, which leads to my home!" Miltin called excitedly.

"We must be near then!" Aska cried. "When do you think we should reach there?"

Miltin did a loop in the air. "In a couple of hours at the latest," he whooped. But as he flipped upright again, a sudden pain seized him, causing his left wing to buckle. He dropped down.

"Miltin!" Aska gasped. She dived after him. Fortunately the robin landed safely on the deck of a boat, the *Rippledew*, which was passing by. Aska came down beside him, steadying him with a wing.

The skipper of the boat came behind them. "Ahoy there, Miltin!" he called merrily. "Looks like you need a ride to the Waterthorn, eh? I hope you haven't forgotten me."

Miltin turned around. "Why, can it be . . ." His eyes widened in surprise. "Quaykkel Lekkyauq!"

"You got that right!" exclaimed the gray duck. He noticed Miltin's bandages and asked, "Are you wounded, Miltin?"

"Nothing serious, thanks," he murmured.

The duck looked skeptical. "You've had some adventures; that's clear," he said. "Well . . . it's noontime, so why don't you have lunch with me and tell me what's been happening to you?"

"Oh, wonderful!" Miltin perked up. He felt as if he hadn't eaten a meal for ages.

They went to the galley and ate plum puddings and spicy salmon stew. Over the meal Miltin told the skipper about Turnatt, his escape, and the need for a Leasorn gem.

As he spoke, a sudden shiver rippled through Miltin. He winced as the movement triggered pains all over his body. The aid from Swordbird's magical flower was waning. He coughed and pretended to choke on the stew. It didn't fool Aska. She shot him a look, but Miltin turned his head away.

After lunch Aska and Miltin went back outside to the deck. She peered closely at his bandages and gasped as she saw a new patch of red soaking through the white linen around the robin's shoulder. "Miltin, are your wounds worse?" she demanded.

"No. I'm—I'm fine."

"I don't think you're telling me the truth," Aska said quietly.

Miltin gazed into the distance. "You're right," he said slowly. "I'm not. If I had let you know the truth, you'd have insisted on stopping to nurse me. But it won't matter if I let you know now, since we're so close to my home."

He paused and sighed. "My wounds can't be healed. All those days of being a slavebird have worn my body down." His head shot up; his eyes filled with anger. "Aska, you can't possibly imagine how I was tortured at Fortress Glooming, for you've never experienced the cruel whip lashings, the painful beatings."

"I know, Miltin. I can't imagine how it must have been," Aska whispered.

Miltin lowered his gaze. "You see, Aska . . .whenever I think of saving Stone-Run and my fellow slavebirds, I forget all my pain."

Just at that moment Quaykkel came over. "Ho, Miltin, I've dropped by to tell you we're at the Waterthorn!" he called. Miltin's face lit up when he turned his head and saw the familiar, beautiful woods not far ashore.

He and Aska thanked Quaykkel and bade him

farewell. They headed toward Miltin's home.

Miltin flew over the shore that he knew so well, his heart pounding. *Mother! Father! Where are you?* he called in his heart. Aska followed, trying to catch up. She thought it strange that Miltin was able to fly so fast all of a sudden. The joy of seeing his home must have given him new strength.

Miltin turned back to point out a place to Aska. "See that, Aska? It's my home!" he called eagerly. Aska looked ahead. At the end of the meadow of red blossoms was a verdant grove of maples, flashing all shades of green. Silhouettes of birds were visible among the trees; songs could be heard faintly.

Just as they landed at the edge of the grove, a few robins hurried out. "Look, it's Miltin! Miltin!" They clustered around him, chattering with excitement. Two of them dashed back to the trees to tell Miltin's parents, all the while shouting to every other bird, "Miltin's back! Miltin's back!"

The whole Waterthorn tribe gathered around Miltin at his parents' nest house. Before he got to the door, his parents were already there, greeting him with tears in their eyes.

Miltin dipped his head. "I'm back, Mother, Father," he said.

Miltin's mother quickly helped him up. "I'm not dreaming, am I, my son? Let me take a closer look at you . . ." she murmured lovingly. "Goodness! Why are you wearing bandages? Are you wounded?"

His father, Reymarsh, helped him through the door. "Let's go into the room first, Miltin. You must be tired."

After they had settled comfortably on cushions, Miltin spoke. "Mother, Father, this is Aska, of Stone-Run Forest. She is here to ask if she can borrow our Leasorn gem."

"What happened? That hawk again?" Reymarsh quickly asked with grave concern.

"The hawk Turnatt made me and the other captives slavebirds at his fortress in Stone-Run. He also attacked Aska's tribe and other birds there. They need our help. Father, you must lead your troops to Stone-Run with the Leasorn tomorrow."

"Tomorrow?"

"Yes, or it'll be too late. Turnatt will attack Aska's tribe."

There was silence. "You need a good rest," Reymarsh said in a low voice. "And you know the ritual didn't work perfectly. Swordbird didn't stay long enough, and we don't know why."

"Promise me you will go tomorrow . . ." Miltin begged.

Reymarsh nodded slowly. Miltin faintly smiled. He opened his beak as if to say something more but suddenly collapsed.

The room was in a turmoil. Miltin's mother called his name again and again. The medicine bird quickly came. "Miltin is in danger, I'm afraid," he reported gravely after an examination.

Miltin's mother burst into tears. "How can you be in such a state, Miltin?" she wailed. "You were healthy and well before you were captured! How can you be so sick after just over a month?"

"Madame, you need to be calm. Let Miltin rest," the medicine bird said.

After a few hours Miltin's eyelids fluttered and opened a crack, revealing his dry and tired eyes. He did nothing but breathe raspingly for a long time. His head spun with dizziness and pain, and he could hardly see anything but numerous spots before his eyes. He felt as if his whole body were in a bonfire.

The flower sent by Swordbird had helped him, he realized. But it couldn't heal him. All Swordbird had been able to do was to give him strength to reach home and complete his mission. "Thank you, Swordbird," he whispered faintly.

“Miltin! Miltin!” He heard Aska calling his name. He was not sure where Aska was. She seemed to be far off. . . .

A warm, unfamiliar feeling enveloped him. No. He could not just let it come. Miltin tried his hardest to speak, but his throat was too dry for him to utter a clear word. His first attempt ended in a round of terrible coughs and hacks. But soon he managed a small, weak whisper.

“A-Aska . . .” he croaked. “I cannot go on to bring my slavebird friends to freedom. Please complete the task for me. You are a powerful, determined blue jay, and I choose you to finish it. Soon I will die. I wish I would see Turnatt be destroyed and the slavebirds go free, through your eyes.” He paused just a little and attempted a smile. The strange feeling once again tried to swallow him. He turned to his parents. “Father! Please fly with Aska, to Stone-Run. . . . Turnatt must be destroyed. . . .” His voice grew barely audible. “I love you, Mother and Father. . . .”

The strange feeling came a third time to take him away. This time Miltin did not struggle to keep it off. He let the warmness go through his whole body; he felt as if he were soaring. A burst of brilliant colors filled his vision. They soon merged into a shade of blood red. The red turned into black. Miltin felt as if he were flying through a dark tunnel. The tunnel seemed endless, full of twists and turns. He was not afraid; he ventured on.

He shot through the opening of the tunnel and into the sky. Miltin's wings no longer hurt, his chest and back no longer ached, and he felt happy and free. Looking behind, he could see his body lying in the nest bed. Around it were his parents, Aska, and his tribe friends. They were crying. All the Waterthorn birds were crying. He hovered in the air for a minute, gazing at them, carving all of them into his memory. "Good-bye, Mother and Father. Good-bye, Aska. Farewell, Waterthorn," he whispered, tears in his eyes. After a while he reluctantly turned and flew toward the skyline, till his tribe was no longer visible in the distance. He flew higher and did loops in the air. Higher and higher he went, until he was flying next to the sun.

"He's gone, gone to Sky Land," whispered Reymarsh, gazing sadly at the still form. He leaned on the hilt of his sword, trying to hold back his tears. "Turnatt, you'll pay!"

Miltin's mother sobbed. Aska, with tears streaming down her cheeks, steadied and comforted her.

Aska sorrowfully looked at the robin's peaceful features. Miltin had a little smile on his face. The afternoon breeze ruffled his feathers. He seemed to be asleep, dreaming of wonderful things. He could live in his dreams forever.

Rest in peace, Miltin, Aska thought. *I will fulfill your wish.*

The wind blew softly over the maples, as if in mourning.

The next day Reymarsh and his tribesbirds held a funeral for Miltin and planted blue flowers on the grave. After that the robin leader readied his troops and took out the red Leasorn. They flew toward Stone-Run with Aska in the lead, chanting furiously, "Down with Turnatt! Set the slavebirds *free*!"

Preparedness may avert danger.

—FROM THE *OLD SCRIPTURE*

20
PREPARATIONS

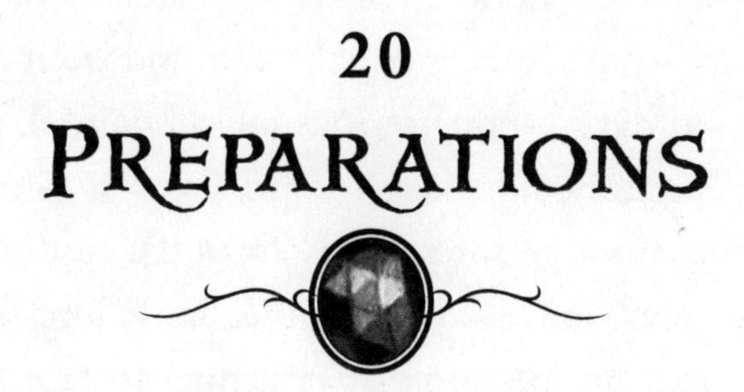

Turnatt waited for Shadow's return, eager to hear of the destructions of the cardinals' camp.

Those little woodbirds killed a score of my best soldiers, he thought. *I'll see them destroyed!* To pass the time, he idly turned the pages of the *Book of Heresy*, although he knew every paragraph by heart. "Defiance spreads like a plague," he murmured to himself, quoting his favorite passages. "Let no one oppose you, even for a second. Crush them before thoughts of rebellion can spread."

But Shadow had been left with no archers or scouts, half a cape, some patches of bald skin, and wounds from arrows and darts—none serious but all painful. He was winging his way, not back toward Fortress Glooming, but deeper into the forest, away from the cardinals and the blue jays and away from the hawk lord as well. Shadow had no intention of returning to face Turnatt and confess his failure.

First there was that strange incident at the Waterthorn tribe, he mused as he flew. *Then those cardinals and blue jays defeated Slime-beak, and now even I could not conquer them. Turnatt's fortune is changing,* the raven decided. *He's no longer a lord I wish to serve.*

The deep shadows of the midnight forest swallowed the raven, and nobird could tell where he had gone.

Glenagh sat in the hall of the cardinals' main tree, bandages wound around his head. In front of him was the *Old Scripture* of the cardinals.

In the margin of the last page of the *Old Scripture,* Glenagh noticed some words: "The first verse will make Swordbird appear; the second will make him stay long enough. The first verse is in this book; the second will be from your heart. Express your wishes there."

Glenagh stared at the page, his heart thumping excitedly. Here was the key. At last he knew what was needed to bring Swordbird and make him stay. He dipped his quill pen in the inkwell and started to write quickly on a fresh piece of paper.

Aska, Reymarsh, and his tribe fighters pushed on with their journey to Stone-Run during the night. They passed the White Cap Mountains quite smoothly, avoiding the Sklarkills by traveling in darkness. In the morning they soon passed the border and entered Stone-Run.

"I'm in your embrace again, dear Stone-Run," Aska murmured happily. She forgot all the hardships on the journey and sped up, flying faster and faster.

The shortest way of getting to the Bluewingle camp was to pass the cardinals' home first. So Aska, Reymarsh, and his robins headed there. Before they drew near, some cardinals darted out. "You're back, Aska!" they cried.

Aska introduced Reymarsh and the robins to them, and the birds talked while they flew.

"Where's Miltin?" one of the cardinals asked.

Everybird became sad and silent at the question, especially Reymarsh, whose face filled with grief. Aska said in a low voice, "He had been too seriously wounded at Fortress Glooming, and we were attacked in the mountains as well. He passed away not long after he reached home."

The birds fell silent, mourning.

After a while Aska broke the silence. "How's my tribe?"

"We have bad news, Aska," a cardinal answered with his head bowed. "Your tribe trees were burned by Turnatt's birds."

Aska gasped in horror. "Have birds taken the flight to Sky Land?"

"Only a few, may Swordbird bless their souls. The rest are living with us now. Come and see them."

Before the cardinal finished his sentence, they had already landed on the threshold of the Sunrise camp. Flame-back, Skylion, Glenagh, and others greeted them warmly, welcoming them inside.

Reymarsh took the red Leasorn gem out of his tunic. "Here's the Leasorn that you urgently need," he said, passing the gem to Flame-back. "With it, and the 'Song of Swordbird,' the great Swordbird can be called."

Flame-back accepted the Leasorn and gingerly held it close to his eyes, examining it. The multifaceted gem was translucent and bright, and it seemed as though there were countless crystal windows inside. When Flame-back turned it slowly, it gave off gleaming red sparks. Everybird gathered around the gem in awe.

"Have you got the 'Song of Swordbird'?" Reymarsh asked Flame-back and Skylion.

Skylion turned his head to Glenagh.

"Yes." Glenagh nodded.

Reymarsh said, "Last time, when my tribe called for Swordbird, Swordbird didn't stay long enough after he appeared. We don't know what we did wrong. I only hope things will be different for your tribe."

"I believe so," Glenagh began with enthusiasm. "I found the instructions for the second verse of the 'Song of Swordbird' in the most unexpected place." He held up a piece of paper.

"A second verse!" Reymarsh cried. "I've never heard of it."

"You're right," Glenagh explained. "If we make the second verse ourselves, and it comes from our hearts, then Swordbird will not just appear but stay. I've finished the second verse. Here."

Reymarsh read it eagerly. "Great. It's well written. Let's make some more copies for everybird."

"Don't forget us!" a loud voice sang out. Lorpil, standing nearby, had been listening. "If there is music involved, the Willowleaf Theater must play and sing. We have our professional pride, you know."

Skylion laughed and promised to get copies of the music to the theater birds. "But where should we put the gem during the ritual, Reymarsh?"

"Well, when we did it, we first put the gem on a platform. But realizing the danger of its getting snatched away by the enemy birds, we let a tribesbird carry it in his beak. It's dangerous work," Reymarsh said. "That bird could easily become a target for the enemy."

"Let me hold the Leasorn during the ritual. I'm not afraid," Aska said quietly.

Glenagh patted her back. "You've done a lot for

Stone-Run, young lass. You should rest a bit."

"I need to fulfill Miltin's last wishes." Aska dipped her head. Everybird became silent when they heard this.

As Aska left the meeting room, she saw a blue jay standing in front of her. He held a red rose held in his claw, the first rose blossom of the year.

"It's you, Cody. What a surprise!" Aska exclaimed.

"This flower is for you, our heroine," Cody said sincerely, and handed the rose to Aska.

When Turnatt realized that Shadow was not going to return, he was so angry that he slammed the *Book of Heresy* shut. He shook his wings and screeched his rage so loud that it made everybird's ears in Fortress Glooming ring for several seconds.

He would no longer send his captain and soldiers to do this job, Turnatt decided. He would lead an attack against the woodbirds himself.

They stared through the splendor of the lights,
through the clouds of faint colors that veiled
the sky, for they knew behind them,
he was here, finally here.

—FROM A STORY IN THE *OLD SCRIPTURE*

21
SWORDBIRD!

The afternoon sun lazily shone on the cardinals' camp. Everything seemed to be calm, but the birds were still wary. They knew Turnatt would not leave them alone for long.

A young cardinal on watch poked his head out of a tree but suddenly drew back in terror. "Turnatt's coming! He's got an army of crows and ravens to attack us!"

Surprise and alarm spread among the woodbirds in the

blink of an eye. Everybird pushed aside leaves to get a better view. There they were, in the southern sky, a dark speck leading a flow of smaller specks, coming closer and closer.

"Get our troops ready!"

"Where's the Leasorn gem? Give it to me!"

"I'll pass the song sheets!"

Reymarsh boomed in his deep voice, "Everybird, prepare for battle! Quick!" Soon about 80 woodbirds prepared to greet Turnatt's 130 or more crows and ravens. The cardinals, blue jays, and robins pulled out their weapons. They formed a circle around the cardinals' camp with their backs to the tribe trees. Some were stationed in the air; others were on the ground. The woodbirds raised their weapons as the leaders of the red, the blue, and the robins roared their war cries simultaneously.

"Power of the sun! Sunrise, charge!" the cardinals shouted.

"Attack! Bluewingles forever!" the blue jays yelled.

The robins did not miss a beat. "Death to the enemies! Waterthorn, fight!"

The war cries enraged Turnatt. "Go on and yell for all you're worth," he growled. He ordered his captain to send out attack signals. Turnatt's soldiers rushed at the defending birds, who braced themselves to hold their line and keep the attackers off. Arrows flew. Birds screamed in pain. They battled in the air, wings and swords flashing. But the defenders were outnumbered. They could not hold out forever.

Aska, Glenagh, Cody, and the theater members flew as quickly as they could to the top of the main camp tree. Aska held the Leasorn gem in her beak, and the theater birds brought their instruments to play the song. Dilby played the harmonica, Kastin the flute, and Mayflower the clarinet. Alexandra plucked the harp, Parrale tapped a small drum, and Lorpil shook the maracas. Cody, leading the song, turned his face to the blue sky:

There's a place we know that holds peace.
There's a time we know that treasures peace.
There's a reason we know why we want peace.
There's a bird we know who can create peace.
Swordbird, Swordbird!
Oh, let us have peace.
Oh, let us have freedom once more.
Let the evil be driven away.
Let the forest be filled with sunshine.
Make the land a peaceful place once more.
May peace and freedom be with birds forever.

The others followed his example, and soon they were all singing their hearts out. The song was so touching that the air trembled at it; the song was so magical that the trees swayed with it.

The theater members played with so much emotion that they were lost in the music. Never before had they played so well. The red Leasorn in Aska's beak shone brighter and brighter, more and more beautiful with every note. From the gem, countless beams of red light streaked out to the sky, as if awaiting the arrival of Swordbird. Aska raised her head high. The blinding light was unbearable, but she remained motionless with her eyes closed. *Swordbird! Come to Stone-Run, Swordbird!* she thought over and over.

The song increased in volume at every note, and it seemed as if the whole forest could hear it. It encouraged the woodbirds and frightened the crows and ravens. The words about peace and freedom made the woodbirds stronger and more courageous. The crows and ravens began to falter.

Turnatt was a little troubled by the singing, but he told himself again and again, "Don't listen to that rubbish song!"

The hawk lord turned to his captain, Slime-beak. "Get those soldiers back to fighting!" he bellowed. "Pay no attention to that song!"

The captain hurried away. To calm his uneasiness, the hawk joined the fighting. Whomever he met, he killed, but each woodbird was braver than the last.

As soon as the final note of the first verse faded into the air, the sky grew darkish gray. It became grayer, and grayer . . . and *flash!* There was never so bright a light, so intense that all the birds couldn't help closing their eyes. It seemed for a second that everything in the forest was as white as new snow. Nothing happened to the woodbirds and the theater birds, but some of the soldiers of Fortress Glooming screamed as their visions became dark forever.

A small whirlwind appeared in the center of the sky. The wind sucked in clouds and soon developed into a spiral of bright colors—glowing rose red, soft golden yellow, lush spring green, vivid peacock blue, and elegant violet. The colors seemed alive, moving, mixing, and changing. Sparkles glistened from the whirlwind as it picked up speed, like small stars dancing in the dark. The winds grew stronger and stronger, strong enough to blow the crows and ravens right off the ground. They struggled, flapped, and yelled. But they were sucked into the whirlpool of colors and never seen again.

Strangely, the wind did nothing to the woodbirds or

the theater members. They stood still, watching the wonder unfold before their eyes.

But Turnatt didn't get the title of tyrant for nothing. He was a sly hawk. Seeing the wind grow stronger, he sneaked away from the battleground and into a cave. He didn't realize that in this cave huddled the red and the blue. Fortunately for the woodbirds in the cave, the hawk didn't venture very far inside. He stayed in the entrance, observing the sky and the cardinals' camp.

Suddenly a streak of forked lightning lit up the whole forest. An earsplitting roll of thunder followed, a sound that vibrated along the grounds and made the tall trees shake. When the lightning faded away into the misty air, there hovered an enormous white bird holding a gleaming sword. *Swordbird!*

The bird had flashing eyes and a light-built frame. He seemed like a gigantic dove at first sight, with dark orbs, a red bill, and scarlet feet. Yet he was different from a dove. He had the gentleness and grace of a swan, the nobility and speed of an eagle, though he was three times larger than the two added together. His wingspan resembled a pale spread of clouds, fanning above the forest.

Swordbird's dazzling sword looked like a sleek silver dragon, and the Leasorn embedded on the hilt was the dragon's eye. The "dragon" sparkled with a myriad of rich, colorful ripples that intertwined with the red rays from the gem in Aska's beak.

Through the glare of the Leasorn light, Aska could see the guardian of peace, Swordbird. Her heart swelled with joy. *Swordbird*, she thought, *you're really here.* Swordbird smiled at her, and she beamed back.

Glenagh's beak fell open in awe. He quickly adjusted his spectacles in order to have an even clearer look at the white bird. *That lean, muscular figure, that magnificent sword, and those feathers of shimmering whiteness. Precisely like the descriptions in the Old Scripture,* thought Glenagh, amazed.

Skylion, Flame-back, and the rest of the woodbirds and the theater birds thought of all the Swordbird stories Glenagh had told them before. It was hard to believe that Swordbird—the wonderful, holy Swordbird from those tales—was truly here.

After playing the interlude, Cody and the singers began the second verse of the song.

Where there is peace there is love,
Where there is peace there is friendship,
Where there is freedom there is happiness,
Where there is freedom there is joy.
Peace and freedom! Peace and freedom!

Oh, we shall ever rejoice,
Oh, we shall ever be thankful
When peace and freedom ring true.
The freedom fighters shall not have died in vain,
The evil shall be punished.
Oh, Swordbird, please give us hope
In the times of darkness.
May Stone-Run be a wonderful forest again.

Turnatt, crouching in the cave, almost fainted from fear. This was the second time in his life he had seen Swordbird. He tried to back away, but his legs didn't work. So he leaned against the mouth of the cave, peering at the sky. Aha! He saw a blue jay on one of the camp trees, with a shining thing in her beak. *It must be that thing that made Swordbird appear! If I wrest it away, Swordbird will vanish,* Turnatt thought. He was just about to rush out to Aska but hesitated. *Swordbird will probably kill me if I go out. I'd better remain hidden here.*

In the darkness Turnatt couldn't see the other birds in the cave, but they could see him, silhouetted against the light from the entrance. They held their breath. Some of the birds who were able to walk carefully picked up some spears, waiting for an opportune moment to throw them at Turnatt.

Swordbird spread his wings even wider and headed for the cave. Turnatt shrank back. Just at that moment he heard a whistling noise behind him, the sound of something being thrown. The next thing he knew, a sharp spear struck his rear end, and several others brushed by. Without thinking, he leaped forward, almost flying into Swordbird.

Swordbird waved his sword and pointed it at Turnatt. Turnatt dipped his head to avoid its shiny beams. He heard Swordbird talking to him in his mind.

You, hawk! The last time I saw you, you were enslaving birds at the Waterthorn. I blinded your left eye and gave you a chance to give up vice. But you threw it away. You came to Stone-Run, built Fortress Glooming, stole more eggs, and caught more woodbirds. Now your day of doom has come!

"No! No! Mercy, Swordbird!" Turnatt begged, bowing down before the terrifying white bird. But his single yellow eye darted cunningly about. Swordbird frowned and shook his head but lowered his sword a little. Turnatt seized his chance. He leaped up from the ground and, flapping his wings furiously, rushed at Aska.

Aska wasn't afraid. She held the Leasorn higher as she took out her saber and pointed it at Turnatt. Cody leaped forward, ready to defend her.

But before Turnatt got close, the sword of Swordbird

sparkled with brilliance. Turnatt instantly burst into flame. A screech of horror came from the ball of fire as it dropped to the ground.

"Turnatt's dead! Turnatt's dead!" the woodbirds cheered.

Swordbird came low, hovering above their heads. He smiled and spoke to them in their minds.

Turnatt is no more. Enjoy freedom and peace again. Peace is wonderful; freedom is sacred. As long as there is peace and freedom, there is tomorrow. Farewell, friends.

I will always watch over you.

Swordbird beat his immense wings, flying higher and higher until he was no more than a white spot in the gray sky. The woodbirds and theater birds flew after him for a while, waving and calling good-bye.

Gradually the sky turned blue, and a rainbow hung in the air, a rainbow that promised peace.

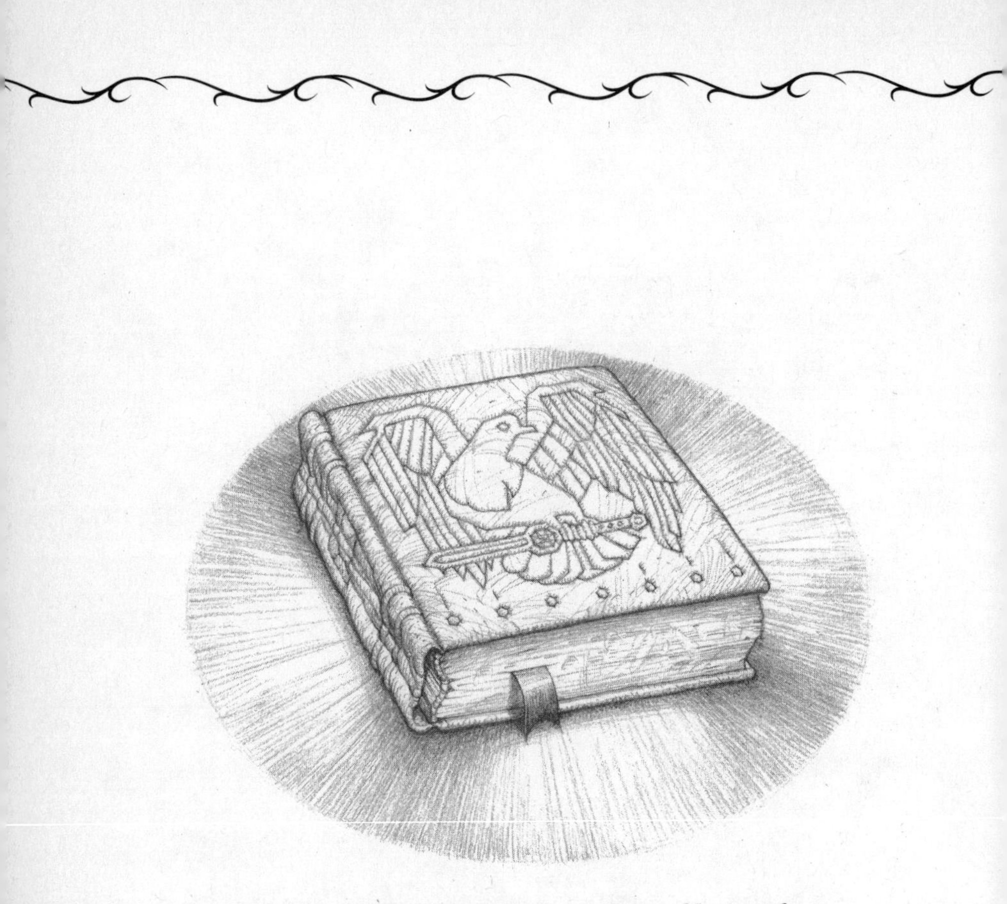

No joy can be compared to that of being free.

—FROM THE *OLD SCRIPTURE*

22
FREEING THE SLAVEBIRDS

When evening came, a party of birds—robins, blue jays, cardinals, and theater members—appeared in the sky above Fortress Glooming.

"Free the slavebirds! Free the slavebirds!" they chanted, waving their weapons in rhythm.

Hearing this, the soldiers who had been left in Fortress Glooming became frightened and uncertain.

Turnatt must've lost the battle, they reasoned, *or else how can the woodbirds come here?*

"If Lord Turnatt is dead, then what's the purpose of staying here? Waiting for death? I'd rather flee!" one of the soldiers cried.

Still uncertain of Turnatt's fate, the remaining crows and ravens flew over the fortress walls and toward the mountains.

When the woodbirds landed on the fortress's ground, they heard voices. "Over here! Over here!" the slavebirds yelled from the compound.

The woodbirds pried open the compound door and rushed inside. There was much hugging and crying. When Reymarsh saw the slavebirds he called to his tribesbirds, "Quick, remove their chains!"

While their bonds were being cut off, the slavebirds couldn't help wincing and crying out in pain. The pieces of metal had worn into their flesh, almost embedded in their skin. But they were so glad.

The slavebirds were free; they were slavebirds no longer. During their celebration they seemed to remember something. "Come with us!" they said, and led the woodbirds to a hut outside. The woodbirds broke into the hut and went inside to inspect. The food before their eyes shocked them.

"Aren't these apples, pine seeds, raisins, and roots ours?" Fleet-tail gasped.

"These walnuts, honey, mushrooms, and raspberries are from my tribe!" said Brontë in anger.

"These are the eggs stolen from the blue jays!" Cody exclaimed.

"Look, those are our cardinals' eggs! We should carry them back. Maybe they'll still hatch," said a cardinal.

All the birds moved the food to the fortress meeting hall, preparing for a feast.

The crystal chandelier in the hall was beautiful when they lit the candles on it. When the birds of the Willowleaf Theater began to play music, everybird started to dance and sway. Their hearts fluttered with the notes. In the air and on the ground the birds danced gracefully, finally at peace.

On one side of the dance floor, Skylion, Flame-back, Glenagh, Reymarsh, Dilby, and Tilosses stood together, talking.

"My tribesbirds and I are leaving tomorrow," Reymarsh said.

"So soon?" Flame-back was surprised. "Why, you can rest a day or two in Stone-Run."

"No, when I left, I was in a hurry. There are still

many things that need to be settled," Reymarsh replied firmly.

"We are traveling south too," Dilby cut in. "Our theater balloon has just been fixed, so we can journey together."

Glenagh looked worried. "What about the freed slavebirds? They can't fly so soon."

Dilby smiled. "Don't worry," he said. "Some of them can travel in our hot-air balloon."

"Besides, the slavebirds who are unable to fly can stay in Stone-Run to rest and heal their wounds," Flame-back offered. "They can leave whenever they want to, or they can settle here."

Skylion nodded in agreement. "Right. Stone-Run's a big place; there's room for everybird."

"Thank you all for your help and generosity. Our debt for your saving our lives can never be paid," Tilosses exclaimed.

The other five smiled at him. "Let's thank Swordbird," Glenagh said, gesturing with both wings to the sky.

Early the next dawn, when the morning glow dyed Stone-Run Forest red, the theater balloon had already started to rise up into the air. In the basket there were also freed slavebirds beside the theater members.

Reymarsh and his robins flew on either side of the balloon.

There were calls of good-bye both from above and below.

A new day began in Stone-Run.

23
Excerpt from the *Stone-Run Chronicles*

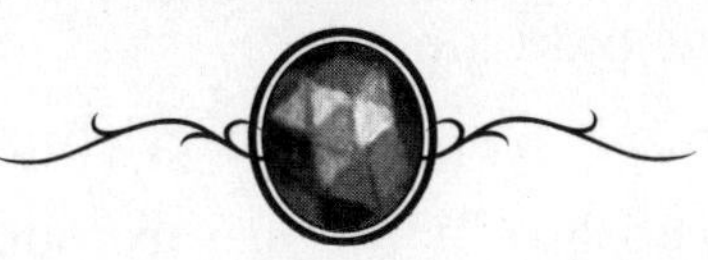

—Excerpt from page 312, Volume XVIII, of the *Stone-Run Chronicles*

It has been about eight seasons since Swordbird came and removed Turnatt from Stone-Run. Whenever our youngsters see a rainbow, they run up to me and take me outside to see it. They ask me whether it is the same as the Swordbird Rainbow and beg me to tell them the stories about Swordbird. Of course the Swordbird

Rainbow is different from any others: You can see it move from one end of the sky to the other, like a shooting star.

The freed slavebirds are happy again. Most of them have returned home, but some have stayed with us. Fortress Glooming has been made into the Stone-Run Library. Now Stone-Run is indeed a wonderful place.

The wedding of Cody and Aska is soon to be held. Of course, as one can expect, most of our youngsters during the days of Turnatt have already had children. It shocks me to think how old I am.

In two days we are going to celebrate the Feast of Peace and Friendship at our camp (south of Fortress Glooming). Everybird is busy preparing for it. The cardinals and we have joined together, and we call ourselves the Stone-Run Forest tribe. The Waterthorn birds and many friends from far away are invited to celebrate the festival. It just warms one's thoughts to think of all the delicious food that will be prepared.

This is a short summary of what has happened since Turnatt perished. The temptation of a freshly brewed cup of acorn tea is too great for me to resist; I will put an end to this entry.

To conclude, I would like to quote Swordbird's words: "Peace is wonderful; freedom is sacred."

Glenagh, Head of the Stone-Run Library

EPILOGUE

A Pool of Liquid Gold

Aska and Cody landed halfway up the hill. "There. There it is," Aska whispered softly, pointing.

Cody nodded, looking at the top of the hill. "Yes, it's just like what you told me, Aska. A dot of white in the midst of the blue sky and the blue flowers. I can even see the bluets, forget-me-nots, and gentians around it."

Aska tried to smile through her tears. "Yes. It hasn't

changed for seasons; it's just the way it was then." She sniffed as memories flooded her head. "I remember that day as if it were yesterday. . . ." She started to cry.

Cody put a wing around her shoulders. "Now, now, Aska. You know we shouldn't stop when we're halfway there. Come on!"

The two blue jays once again flew. They fluttered a short distance and landed on the hilltop. The late-afternoon wind's breath stirred the flowers and grass by the grave, making small rustling noises. The two birds let their eyes slowly sweep over the inscription on the headstone.

MILTIN SILQUORE

A loving son, an honest friend,
and a true warrior who came home
despite troubles and hardships.
He sacrificed his life to help others
and will be remembered forever.

The words were slightly worn from rain and wind, but they were still distinct. The marble headstone glistened in the fading light. Aska stood there motionless. Tears blurred her vision as she remembered the cheerful, smiling robin.

Aska sniffed. "Miltin," she whispered, "I am back. I have seen Swordbird; I have seen the tyrant Turnatt die; I have seen the slavebirds happy and free. I hope, through my eyes, you saw them too." She brushed away a tear and smoothed her feathers as the wind changed direction. "Miltin, I've brought you a gift, a gift that can only mean peace." Aska took a package out of her pack. She carefully unwrapped the cloth. "A feather, Miltin. It is not any ordinary feather. It is Swordbird's. This I give you, Miltin. Rest in peace." She inserted the beautiful feather into the ground among the blue flowers.

Aska stepped back to look. The snow white feather seemed to make the blue of the flowers even brighter. It brought an almost lively look to the tombstone. *Miltin would like that,* Aska thought.

Cody stood at the gravestone. He wanted to say many things but could only utter a few. "Brother Miltin, I represent Stone-Run to thank you. We will never forget that you saved our lives. Rest in peace."

The two blue jays remained at the grave for a long time before they took off. After flying for a few seconds, Aska looked back. Her sadness changed into joy, for she saw that the feather of Swordbird made the tombstone sparkle. She had never seen such a beautiful scene. The setting sun's rays shimmered on the flowers and the tombstone, gilding the blue and white colors until they seemed like a pool of liquid gold.

Major Characters

Alexandra—hummingbird, a member of the flying Willowleaf Theater, harpist.

Aska—blue jay, a member of the Bluewingle tribe, cousin of Brontë, and, later, the wife of Cody.

Bone-Squawk—crow, cook of Fortress Glooming.

Brontë—blue jay, a member of the Bluewingle tribe.

Bug-eye—crow, slave driver of Fortress Glooming.

CODY—blue jay, a member of the Bluewingle tribe, and, later, the husband of Aska.

CROOKED-SHOULDER—crow, a gate guard of Fortress Glooming.

DILBY—loon, a member of the flying Willowleaf Theater, plays harmonica and violin.

FLAME-BACK—cardinal, leader of the Sunrise tribe.

FLEA-SCREECH—crow, a soldier of Fortress Glooming, slave catcher.

FLEET-TAIL—cardinal, a member of the Sunrise tribe.

GLENAGH—blue jay, a member of the Bluewingle tribe, a respected elder, bookkeeper, expert in the ancient language, and, later, head librarian of the Stone-Run Library.

GLIPPER—flycatcher, a slavebird of Fortress Glooming.

KASTIN—tufted titmouse, a member of the flying Willowleaf Theater, flutist and pianist.

LARGE-CAP—crow, a gate guard of Fortress Glooming.

LORPIL—gannet, a member of the flying Willowleaf Theater, comedian, plays the maracas.

MAYFLOWER—junco, a member of the flying Willowleaf Theater, clarinetist and pianist.

MILTIN SILQUORE—robin, a slavebird of Fortress Glooming, a member of the Waterthorn tribe, son of Reymarsh.

PARRALE—wood duck, a member of the flying Willowleaf Theater, drummer.

QUAYKKEL LEKKYAUQ—duck, skipper of the *Rippledew*.

REYMARSH—robin, leader of the Waterthorn tribe, father of Miltin.

SHADOW—raven, scout of Fortress Glooming.

SKYLION—blue jay, leader of the Bluewingle tribe.

SLIME-BEAK—crow, captain of Fortress Glooming.

SWORDBIRD (WIND-VOICE)—white bird, guardian of peace, son of the Great Spirit.

TILOSSES—sparrow, an old slavebird of Fortress Glooming.

TURNATT—hawk, lord of Fortress Glooming.

WIND-VOICE—the same as Swordbird.

ACKNOWLEDGMENTS

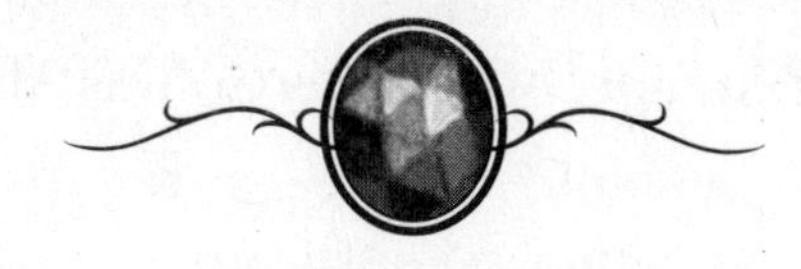

I feel very fortunate that Mother Nature bestowed me a gift, the inspiration for *Swordbird*, when I was a child of ten romping in the deep forests on the hills of Hamilton, New York. With that in mind, along with my deep love for birds and my heart's wish for peace, I sat down in front of the computer and began writing my first novel.

There are many people who helped breathe *Swordbird* into life.

First, I would like to express my heartfelt thanks to Ms. Phoebe Yeh, editorial director of HarperCollins

Children's Books, for spending time on *Swordbird* beyond work hours, magically and painstakingly transforming *Swordbird* into a much better book than its first draft; Ms. Kate Jackson, senior vice president of HarperCollins Children's Books, for taking time to read *Swordbird* and giving me encouragement; Ms. Jane Friedman, president of HarperCollins, for bringing me—a twelve-year-old writer—a ray of hope; Ms. Whitney Manger, editor; Ms. Amy Ryan, art supervisor; Mr. Mark Zug, illustrator; and the rest of the wonderful team at HarperCollins for making *Swordbird* possible.

I also owe many thanks to Mrs. Melissa Barnello, my fantastic fifth-grade teacher; Ms. Judy Wood, my teacher in the Gifted and Talented program; Mr. Barry Guinn, a very kind principal; Ms. Patricia Brigati and the rest of my caring church friends; Ms. Betty Barr, MBE; and Ms. Victoria Theisen, my terrific sidekick. All of them read my first draft of *Swordbird* in whole or in part, and their suggestions and support encouraged me to go further.

Special thanks must be said to Ms. Diane Goodwin, my ESL teacher when I first came to the United States, who lit the spark of literature in my heart; Mr. Timothy Simmons, my third-grade teacher, and Mr. Ben Farstad, my reading-group teacher, for encouraging me to write; Mr. and Mrs. Cleo and Char Kelly, my neighbors and friends, who lent me many classic and award-winning books.

I must thank my parents for their encouragement all the way. And my pet birds, Captain Crackleclaw, Kibbles, and Plap, who cheered me on with their delightful songs.

Without those mentioned, *Swordbird* could never appear on earth!

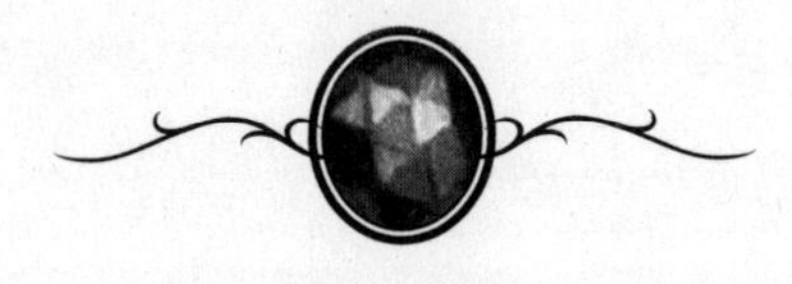